Alan Beaumont's Dilemma

by

Mike Silkstone

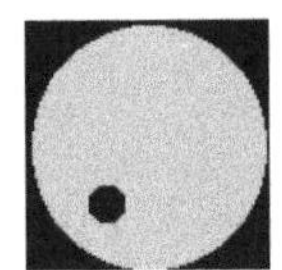

Human Interfaces,
9 Normanby Terrace, Whitby, YO21 3ES, England.

ISBN 978-1-898728-41-2

1 2 3 4 5 6 7 8 9

Also by Mike Silkstone

Published by Undead Tree Publications:

The 'Steeas' Trilogy…
Three Loves
Seasons O' Steeas
Satan Garth

Published by Human Interfaces:

Poetry Anthology…
Gay's The Word!

Contents

To Trevor, Ivan and Monty.

Black diamonds, black diamonds fit for a king
To wear in his crown, sceptre or ring.
Hard helmet, clogs, knee-caps, ready to go,
Miner's lamp in hand, it makes quite a show.
With pick and shovel. Deep down in the earth,
Men dig at the coal-face, for all they're worth.
Black diamonds, black diamonds, the victor's spoils
Where the man among men labours and toils.
Works alongside family, sons and brothers,
Coal-mining bond is stronger than others.
Though the work is hard and the pay is low,
The coal-face beckons, the collier must go.
Black diamonds, black diamonds fit for a King
To wear in his crown, his sceptre or ring.

(The Miner's Lament, Mike Silkstone.)

Chapter 1

He glanced into the driving mirror, and seeing the road behind him clear indicated a right turn before moving toward the centre lane. Traffic lights turned to green and he swung into Challinor Street, a thoroughfare still busy with West Riding housewives anxious to pick up a last-minute bargain from the open air fruit and vegetable market.

The frugality of miners' wives and mill workers!

Still, he reasoned, his own parents were of the same cloth. Nothing in the house was wasted. It seemed a reminder of the war years, when everything was on ration.

His van slowed down then came to a halt as a group of children obviously on their way home from school stood by the pedestrian crossing seeming undecided as to what to do. He waited, they meandered across the road one by one. There was a girl with curly blonde hair, and a spotty faced teenager picking his nose.

Nothing had changed from his own schooldays, and seeing them brought back a sudden image of his last few weeks at secondary-modern. There was Miss Tipler still (even after two years of the same topic) prattling on about 'The Glorious Reign of Elizabeth I' while Charlie Chapman who taught scripture, (or Religious Education, as it was then called) had, one afternoon, a classroom full of fifteen-year-old boys who were about to be let loose into the world of adults and needed preparing and 'guidance' for this, while the girls were being subjected to a similar thing overseen by Miss Sykes, who taught hockey and P.E.

Charlie Chapman seemed more nervous than the innocent faces staring up at him as he started talking about boys growing into young men, and 'things' happening, not just to their minds, but also to their bodies. He began with the Garden of Eden, then somehow managed to get side-tracked and prattled on about wickedness and fornication, and even self-abuse as young men did unspeakable things to the private parts of their bodies to relive and hopefully calm their wanton desires.

It could cause blindness, even madness; whilst submitting to carnal lust and consorting with 'certain women' would, in most cases lead to contracting unspeakable diseases. Any children they might eventually father would be at best, deformed, at worst, absolute idiots.

Not once was that three-letter word mentioned, or even love – and certainly not 'climaxes' or sexual fulfilment. No, these things didn't happen in the gospel according to Charlie Chapman.

Days later, now ready to face the world he turned up for his first morning's work. He was officially a junior reporter, but this 'junior reporting' seemed to be nothing more than making endless cups of coffee as and when required, and running to the bakers a hundred yards down the road.

Some two years later, however, on his seventeenth birthday, and along with Jennifer Taylor, some four or five years his senior and photographer for the weekly *Chronicle,* the two of them were to 'interview' and photograph the owner of the town's repertory theatre which was about to close and be demolished.

She had with her lots of paraphernalia, he had a long list of questions needing to be asked, very politely "Mr Jeffreys will be along shortly" they were informed by a woman who they took to be the cleaner, "he says 'take any pictures that you need – just feel free to roam around.' "

They were in the dress circle standing in one of the boxes at the side of the stage when it happened. Jennifer, pretending she needed to get some shots at a certain angle had him crouched on the floor so that he could also 'view the action' and in no time at all had his jeans and underpants round his ankles.

For days afterwards he'd worried in case he – well, he couldn't hit the jackpot first time trying, but when he saw a job as an apprentice painter and decorator advertised in the situations vacant column, (even though the advert carried a box number as opposed to the name of the firm) he was on the phone that same afternoon.

It was quickly pointed out to him that one usually began an apprenticeship at the age of fifteen… but under the circumstances, for he must be very keen to have contacted them so quickly and without 'going through the proper channels' he could start at the end of the month.

That was, he mentally calculated, in the summer of nineteen fifty-two, and now, six years later he was earning a proper man's wage, and more than most when one took into account the recent overtime and weekends he'd been working – and tomorrow would be pay day again.

The late afternoon sun hit the tip of the Pennines in the far distance, the decorators' van carried on the main Huddersfield-Wakefield road until, reaching Lepton Edge pit, took the next right turn and a mile further along the now country road, and reaching Hob-Cote, which was nothing more than a row of back-to-back two-up one-down miners' cottages, turned right again down to the cluster of houses in Haigh Bottom, little more than a crossroads on the outskirts of the village, and his parents' home. Minutes later he parked outside the stone built cottage, the middle one of three.

The end of a hard day.

"Hallo mam, I'm home," he called out as he opened the inner porch door that led into the kitchen cum living room.

"Aye, cum on lad, yer dinner's all ready."

"Eee, it smells good," he complimented her cooking.

"Better na them mucky overalls yer wearin'. Yer'd best put 'em in 'back o' van, then tuck inter this lot," and a hand pointed to the evening meal. "Yer gran allus said Thursdays were commonsense days, and yer'd ter cook what yer 'ad over thro 'beginnin' o' week. So it's fried 'taties an' onions an' mushy peas, an' ah got a 'am shank this mornin' ter go wi' em."

"That'll suit me."

Gladys Beaumont stroked the front of her wraparound pinnie, then tucked in a strand of hair that had dared to defy her scraped-back hair-do. "An' yer've 'ad a letter thro…" and she paused then took the printed leaflet from the envelope. "Watson's, Decorators' Supplies."

"Oh, it's belonging 'work, I'll take it in wi' me tomorrow mornin'."

"That's all reight then. It's 'ad me an' yer dad worried. We thought when we read it as yer wor thinkin' o' settin' up on yer own."

"No, it's just… mi boss wants to know if a rival firm can offer a better deal than he's getting now, but didn't want to use his own name."

"Oh, ah see. Nah, get aht o' yer work clothes, and get yer 'ands washed, an' then yer can eat."

He looked round, then asked, "Where's mi dad?"

"Up in 'allotment, doin' summatt wi' 'pigeon loft."

"I hope he's nooan painting it. If he does it green he'll have parrots to cope with instead of pigeons" he tried to joke, but his mother seemed suddenly serious.

"An' when yer've 'ad yer dinner ah'm goin' ter call on mi aunt Phoebe. Shu reckons 'er 'ens are layin' fifty ter 'dozen, so shu might sell me sum eggs, yer nivver know."

"Right. I'll more than likely go for a drink later on."

"But not till… well, yer dad wants ter 'ave a talk wi' yer. Man ter man, so ah mun keep out o' road. That's why ah'm catchin' 'alf past six bus, ter give yer booath a bit o' space fer private conversation."

Alarm bells were beginning to sound. A 'man-to-man' talk was something that he'd dreaded ever since leaving school. A father should not, under any circumstances, discuss anything vaguely to do with *that* with his son. Talking about sex was reserved for, and between, those of one's own age.

How could a lad boast of his exploits to his own father? His mates, yes, because they could do likewise, but your own father couldn't tell you what he'd been up to in the bedroom with your mother. It would be… obscene… disgusting!

And the language used in connection with such activity. A lad, even a twenty-three-year-old couldn't use *that* word in front of his dad. With his mates, yes… but not… well, it wasn't on! Unless, of course, it was dad wanting advice

"What's dad… er, got on his mind?"

"Nay, it's between the two o' yer. Nowt ter do wi' me. Now," and she opened the kitchen cabinet, "Tomato ketchup or brown sauce?" She held them, one in each hand, he pointed accordingly.

"And I'll wash up when I've eaten. I'll leave everything tidy."

"That's a good lad. Now, ah'd better get ready. 'Bus'll be due in twenty minutes."

He no longer felt hungry, just sort of… 'queasy' at what might – was going to transpire when William Henry Beaumont came through the door.

Chapter 2

" 'Ad a good day?"

"Mmm. Better outside this weather than stuck in a front room papering a ceiling when there's loads of furniture to move and ornaments and things that might get damaged."

"Oh aye," his father agreed without giving the matter any serious thought. The two men drifted into a mutual silence, each one of them consumed with their own thoughts.

"I'm going for a drink later on," Alan finally spoke. "D'you want me to bring a bottle o' Guinness back?"

"Aye, that'd go dahn a treat," and taking a cigarette from the packet of twenty he then waved them toward his son.

"Thanks, dad."

The elder of the two men took a deep breath to inhale the smoke, went red in the face then coughed as though about to spew his guts up. "Coal dust" was how it was explained away, or even "miner's lung disease" but never emphysema, for that sounded something serious.

"Well… I'll er… put another shirt on and…"

"Aye… er… yer mam an' me , we wor talkin' abaht this an' that… an' one thing led on ter another…"

"Oh aye?"

"An' yer name kept croppin' up. Shu's gettin' fair worried abaht yer, yer know. When that letter arrived for yer this mornin' shu fair 'ad palpitation – ah thought shu were goin' ter 'ave a do."

"Whatever for?"

"Well, it could 'appen ony day nah. Yer twenty-three, yer apprenticeship's over."

"But what's that to do with mum getting worried about me?"

"Dooant yer see? Call-up papers. National Service!"

"Oh that," and he heaved a sigh of relief. "Is that what you wanted to talk about? Mum said there was something, but she wouldn't say what."

"Aye lad. Shu thinks a lot abaht yer. Yer all we 'ave, yer know. If owt 'appened ter yer shu'd nivver get over it. It wor bad enough when yer brother Peter got ta'en ter 'ospital wi' scarletina an' died two days later. Shu still talks abaht 'im, an' time doesn't 'eal, as folks say it does. That's why we can't risk yer goin' in 'army, an' bein' sent ter sum trouble spot in 'world an' gettin' blown ter bits.'"

"Well, that won't happen."

"Yer dooant know that."

"Besides, given the choice, I could... join the navy... or the Air Force."

"Nah that 'ud be a silly thing ter do. Yer ship could sink, an' In a plane yer might get shot dahn. As yer aunt Muriel says, 'if man were meant ter fly 'ee'd 'a' been born wi' a pair o' wings.'"

"But there's no way round this, even if we wanted to find one. National Service is compulsory, it's something every able bodied man has to do. My cousin survived doing his bit for queen and country. Because I was serving an apprenticeship my National Service has been deferred – but not cancelled."

"Oh, ah know that, so does yer mother, an' she accepts what yer sayin'"

"Well then..."

"But there is another way."

"A conscientious objector? I didn't know there still were such individuals. Or could we pretend I'm ready for the funny farm? A little bit missing?"

"No – no no no, yer gettin' it all wrong. 'Answer's starin' yer straight in 'face. Yer need to be in what's called a 'reserved occupation' an' then yer'll nooan get called up."

"Well, I'm not. Being a painter and decorator isn't in that league."

"– But a miner? Workin' dahn 'pit?"

Alan Beaumont suddenly reeled! He stared at his father. Had he gone mad?

"Just think abaht it, lad. Yer'll get proper trainin', not like it wor when I started day after ah left schooil. There's a twelve week course nah for young lads in this area. Six weeks training at Woolley Colliery an' alternate weeks at Barnsley Tech., an' yer get paid while yer trainin'. What d'yer say?"

"Er..." and he pulled a face. "It needs... consideration."

"Well, that's what we want yer ter do. Consider it. An' there's summatt else."

"Oh?"

"Aye. A twenty-three-year-old lad should be thinkin' abaht… well, somebody's 'sweet' on yer."

"Eh?" and alarm bells we're not merely 'ringing' they were pealing full pelt.

"Aye. Yer'll 'appen remember young Mavis Pickersgill? Yer went ter 'same secondary schooil 'Shu's abaht your age, give a year or so."

He racked his brain. The name struck a chord – not a pleasant one.

"Me an' 'er father Frank work on 'same shift. Shu comes off a good family, and Frank says shu's lookin' for a young man wi' serious intentions. Pickergill's are nooan withaht brass, it could be a good match. Shu works in 'mill wi' 'er mother. Shu's a mender."

Menders, spinners, Dobcross loom tuners, shoddy workers, so many times had Alan seen the mill jobs advertised in the situations vacant when he worked for the Chronicle. More such columns than there was actual news, and when he had to travel to work on the early morning bus, well, the mill workers seemed to have the bus to themselves, so very many of them there were. A girl friend who worked in the mill? – or even worse, a wife! No, it was something he didn't – couldn't cope with.

His father was waiting for a reply.

"But… we don't even know one another."

"Well, we could sooin alter that. If all parties were in agreement they could come for afternooin tea next weekend. Yer mam's talkin' abaht a bit o' brisket an' salad, an shu's even offerin' ter mak' a sponge cake an' a trifle ter finish off wi' . Then after we've all 'ad a good tuck in… you an' Mavis could… 'ave a natter, or go for a walk."

"Even go to chapel and hear aunt Ada Martha hit wrong notes when she's playing the organ."

"Shu does 'best shu can, and there's nooan all that many in 'congregation these days. No, 'pews are nearly all empty, 'cept fer weddin's an' funerals."

"But to get back to what you were suggesting earlier," and Alan mercyfully saw a way out of what could become an impossible situation. "Next weekend's the start of Wakes Week, have you forgot? I'll be at the coast."

"Oh, damn an' bugger it! Still, it'll all save till yer get back, there's no rush. An' er… it's also on 'cards as there might be a weddin' present as'll buy a nice little 'ouse. Them terrace properties where 'Pickergills live are they're allus comin' on 'market. There's one fer sale nah two doors away thro where they live. Ah said as they were nooan short on a bob or two, fer yer might remember owd Amos Eastwood as kept *'Travellers' Rest?* Well, 'ee wor related ter Amy Pickersgill, 'ee wor 'er uncle. Bowlegged wi' brass, an' no other livin' relatives. when 'ee dropped deead they copped the lot. Money in 'bank, *'Travellers' Rest* that they sold fer a tidy sum, an' a property next ter 'doctor's surgery they draw rent on ivvery week… an' they've only Mavis, they've no other bairns. Shu'll be a wealthy woman, when owt ails 'er mother an 'father.

The room was becoming claustrophobic, as were thoughts of the new life that his parents were planning for him. He had to escape before it was too late.

He jumped up. "I'm going for a drink."

"But what shall I tell Frank?"

But no answer was forthcoming. His son and heir was running down the garden path.

That which was said to 'knit up the ravelled sleeve of care' was eluding him. Alan Beaumont was a worried young man.

A stint in the army was… well, it happened to lots of other young fellers, some even chose to make it their career, and his fellow workmate and best pal had had a rare old time, even if one believed only half the tales he told. Two years in Germany could be the best two of his life, and even if not, it would soon pass, and seemed as nothing when compared to a lifetime of working on the coal face. Yet he came from a coal-mining family and a coal-mining area, and the village seemed surrounded by pits, There was Lepton Edge, Shuttle-Eye Colliery, Nine-Clogs, (or Capus, as it was called locally) and at

Emley Moor there was Stringers, or Fanny Main. Then there was a pit at nearby Skelmanthorpe, and on the way to Barnsley there was Wooley Colliery. The other side of Barnsley was Houghton Main, then there was Gawber Colliery, and Silkstone Colliery. The whole of the area seemed to be built on some giant coal seam.

In his own village farmers' fields were being plundered, as bulldozers tore away the topsoil and made a droning noise from morn till night. Outcropping, as it was referred to, seeming suddenly infinitely more profitable than dairy farming. Mountains of soil would eventually be complemented by piles of coal – and where would it end? Would the whole area suddenly collapse, just drop into mother earth and be swallowed up?

It was a frightening thought!

No, working down the pit was not for him, he'd have to… well, it just wasn't going to happen – and he suddenly remembered his uncle Ben, mum's youngest brother. His earliest recollection of him was when he came to visit them following the death of his nephew Peter. He brought with him two bars of chocolate, Caley Tray, and some bananas. His mum had stared in near amazement at such gifts, but uncle Ben was, well, he was different!

He had defied 'family' and joined the Air Force and was home on leave – but when the war was over he had to pay the price for his so-called 'cowardice'. For, according to his brothers, 'real men' worked down the pit, he'd taken the easy way out by being a fighter pilot. His three still unmarried collier brothers as a 'protest' now shared the same bedroom, Ben had to sleep on his own, nor would they allow him to sit with them at mealtimes, or stand by the bar next to them in the Working Mens', or have any communication with them, and after a time he sort of 'disappeared' and went to live somewhere the other side of Leeds. No one in the family knew where exactly, nor did they care.

And it also occurred to him – there was a definite 'absence' of any type of military uniform in the village. Lads left school and became 'pen-pushers', then worked in the colliery office as wages clerks. Similarly, local lads who worked at David Browns in Huddersfield, or Brooke Motors or even apprentice electricians, when their apprenticeship was complete they'd be electricians working down the pit – they never seemed to go in the army! He got a silly image of himself painting 'National Coal Board' signs and pit-head fencing, or the outside of the pit manager's office. Something dark green, or maroon, certainly not white.

Then a much worse scenario flashed through his mind. Life with Mavis Pickersgill!

He could just imagine her as she would be now. Plain, and smelling of 'mill'!

Oh, she'd be pure and untouched in *that* department, and even on her wedding night wouldn't know what was expected of her. Besides, he preferred his women older than him, and even if not more experienced, certainly very 'considerate' toward the innocent he pretended to be. They'd look at him in surprise as he'd suddenly be all shy before admitting that he'd 'never done it'. He'd shake his head, saying he'd never seen a girl without her clothes on, nor had anyone seen or run their hands over his naked body, and his partner, thinking that she was seducing a virgin would feel flattered as she drew him toward her and showed him what love was all about.

It worked every time, he'd got it down to a fine art.

So very different would be married life in a house two doors away from a mother and father-in-law, which his own father was 'tempting' him with – well, it was a recipe for a disaster. But it wasn't going to happen. He had other plans, yet he realised that in West Riding villages and among small communities marriages were still 'arranged'. His mother's sister had married his dad's brother, and because that had seemed a stable relationship and in-laws knew one another, his parents had met socially on family occasions, and two years later were wed. This 'two sided family bonding' had resulted in a cousin who was not quite his brother, but very close, until being separated by him having been to university and 'edicated' as his aunt was quick to point out on every possible occasion.

But aunt Grace was like that, and his uncle Walter? – well, uncle and nephew had an intense dislike, the one toward the other, and his growing from childhood to an adult had in no way lessened the feelings Alan had toward the man who had bullied and ridiculed him on every possible occasion. But now he could give as good back as was thrown at him, and as for him being asked to decorate their house – when hell froze over, perhaps – but not until.

Chapter 3

"You need to get a move on, gentlemen," Rosemary Boothroyd looked at the three young men as she spoke, "because 'she who must be obeyed' could be here any minute, and we don't want to upset her, do we Basil?"

He gave his twin sister a look that spoke volumes. "No. Upsetting mother is the very last thing on our list of jobs this morning."

"Or any other morning," Alan joked.

"Exactly. So come on, the three of you. Quick March."

The son of Boothroyds, Painters and Decorators, gave a sigh. "Right, fellers, let's get to it," and as they trudged into the yard and began loading the van.

Rosemary looked again at her handful of invoices. They'd all have to be in order and neat and tidy before mother arrived, but that would be… well, she'd first call at the bank to collect the money for the wages, and they didn't open till ten, and then she'd probably call and get the *Chronicle* that came out Fridays, and that would give her something to moan about as she scanned the headlines

Fortunately (for her daughter), coming in to do the weekly wages was the only time her dear mother graced the office with her presence. There would also be the weekly accounts and the petty cash and the like to make balance, and when these tasks had been executed her dear mother would be away.

Rosemary glanced at her watch, she must tidy the desk. Now – but more pressing – remove the betting slips. All forms of gambling her mother disliked, for, as she often pointed out "The bookmaker must win, or go out of business."

But despite her disapproval of such activity Lizzie, wearing a man's tweed overcoat regardless of the season or the weather, would call daily to take the men's bets to the local bookie, and also to pay any monies due from the previous days 'speculations', and Rosemary suddenly remembered when her mother, to everyone's amazement put five pounds to win on Sundew running in the Grand National – and the horse romped home and won by eight lengths at twenty to one.

The jockey was Fred Winters, the owner a Mrs G. Kohn, the punter who condescendingly collected her winnings as though they were a mere nothing would soon be gracing the place with her presence.

There were the ledgers to put in place, a list of queries from possible clients and the usual post, and rubbish that seemed to arrive daily. When the office was to her liking, Rosemary Boothroyd heard bombarding her brain a blast of trumpets and 'saw' Archbishops, Lord Mayors and High Court Judges and lesser known members of the Royal Family bowing and prostrating themselves as the driving force and brains behind Boothroyd and Son, Painters and Decorators, made her entrance.

Constance Boothroyd (and she was always quick to correct people who dared to mistakenly refer to her as 'Connie') was a woman with her now-generous frontage draped in purple, a skirt sensibly designed to allow for the pear-shaped figure she seemed to have acquired, and feet squeezed into black patent high-heeled shoes. A sculptured hairstyle and just enough make-up as befitted a lady of taste and refinement rather than a T.A.R.T. or a Madam.

She wore cultured pearls round her neck and in her ears. Nothing flashy or flamboyant, she spoke quality. The only child of the late Councillor Walshaw – a much-respected and popular figure in the town. Two years after her marriage, the union was blessed with twins, a boy and a girl, and having felt that she had now done her wifely duty she was able to devote her time to pursue her great passion in life, for she was not merely a soprano, she was a coloratura. There were Lunchtime Concerts at the Town Hall, and evening Song Recitals together with 'Guest Appearances' with the town's Philharmonic Society where she'd astound her audience with her *Queen of the Night* aria from Mozart's *Magic Flute,* or *The Laughing Song* from Offenbach's *Die Fleidermaus.* There was interest from record companies, even talk about a 'London Debut' at the Wigmore Hall, and adjudicating at local music festivals, or being an examiner for the Associated Board of the Royal School of Music.

The world was her oyster, and (on occasions) even she wondered why she had turned her back on this glittering lifestyle, and settled for nothing more than being the soloist for the local church harvest festivals and carol concerts, and occasional oratorios at both Leeds and Huddersfield Town Hall, and unpaid secretary for a husband whose decorating business was in the doldrums. But there were 'the children' to consider, and motherly duties that had to take priority over what could have been international acclaim – but sometimes, when she 'viewed' her offspring, she questioned her earlier sacrifices.

Her son Basil, after two years in the army, was 'following in father's footsteps' and had been made a junior partner and had also not merely 'developed' but had perfected the art of breaking wind at the most inappropriate times and conspicuous occasions. He was still a bachelor, and she knew – oh, she knew – that unmarried men of that age were quite, quite immoral.

Fortunately, that was a part of his life that he kept from his family, but what he couldn't hide was that he'd recently been banned from driving for eighteen months following an accident (which he failed to report), and that could have caused problems workwise, had it not been for Alan (who had just passed his driving test, but had no car). He was now the 'official driver', and had become a valuable part of Boothroyd and Son.

These two young men seemed to frequent the same dance halls (or 'picking-up places') as she considered them to be, and on these occasions Alan would arrive at their home and, leaving the decorators' van in the driveway, the two men would descend on the town in Basil's car, but with (she hoped) Alan at the wheel.

His twin sister Rosemary (who often piously and ecclesiastically referred to him as 'Brother Fartiarse'), although a pianist with several diplomas to her credit, had not inherited her mother's love for the concert platform, and had never had aspirations to becoming a solo performer, which was a pity, for she could have helped her in so many ways in that department. As yet unmarried. But, Constance told herself, some young solicitor or hospital consultant could appear on the scene – and the sooner the better. Her daughter would be thirty in a couple of months. A year nearer to being 'left on the shelf'.

Children could be such a disappointment in many ways, which was why she had sought consolation in working with the town's Operatic Society. She was on the casting committee, the ladies' committee, and various other things. Boothroyds, Decorators, would also help should special sets or scenery need to be painted for the society's productions, and of course, being such a valuable member of the society, she was treated with great respect and courtesy – the exception to this being the woman who had suddenly appeared on the scene suggesting that she might help the society by supervising chorus routines and ensembles.

She also claimed to be an ex-Bluebell Girl, and in the early years of her career she'd been a dancer in several Noel Coward musicals, and that he'd regarded her as a personal friend. Noel Coward? Knowing the likes of her? And she further claimed that Vanessa Lee and Olive Gilbert were among her close friends. Oh, the cheek of the woman! There seemed to be no end to her blatant lies and exaggerations, but Constance knew – oh, she knew just by looking at her – the profession she'd been associated with. The oldest in the world!

It was so disgustingly obvious, from the dyed hair and garish make-up, the flamboyant clothes, the expensive furs casually draped over her arms whenever she appeared, cavorting like a model on a cat-walk and the cheap. tatty jewellery she flaunted in her efforts to dazzle and impress, and as a certain mark of her calling, the gold chain round her right ankle.

Several times had Constance been tempted to enquire from her town council friends was 'Miss Bluebell' paying business rates on her flat, and had so far resisted the temptation to contact the Inland Revenue in relation to her source of income. That might – would – come later.

And the woman had somehow managed to acquire an entourage of very effeminate young men who danced attendance on her and posed as though part of some bizarre stage routine. One could tell at first glance just what sort of men they were, they were probably also selling their bodies, and she was their mentor. The trollop!

She should be hounded out of the town, she really must have further words with her councillor clique.

“We have friends in very high places,” she’d boast whenever the conversation would allow, but what was the good of that if they were not able to move the baggage on?

No, she would have to do something about it, as soon as the Society’s forthcoming production was out of the way. The members of the council had helped Boothroyds in various ways, she would have to repay them by helping to restore morality and decency to the town by having Miss Bluebell removed. Even husband Stanley had to admit, it did have a certain ‘pull’, the people she knew as far as work was concerned. The business was now flourishing, there was money in the bank, new cars every twelve months, and even holidays abroad, and – and Constance Boothroyd stopped day dreaming – she’d a pile of work to get through. She scrolled her Parker pen on the corner of a piece of foolscap, she didn’t want the ink to suddenly make a mess over her ledger entry.

She glanced at the invoices her daughter had laid out for her inspection, there was much to do – yes, even for a coloratura!

Chapter 4

"Alan," she purred, "do sit down, and let's see… six, no, seven hours overtime?"

"That's correct, Mrs Boothroyd."

"And there's… National Insurance contributions to deduct… and income tax… and that's going to leave us with the grand total…" and she stared over her glasses at him. "My, you're going to be quite a wealthy young man if this continues."

He nodded, knowing the value of bowing and scraping.

"Yes, Mrs Boothroyd."

"I hope you're being sensible, and not… well, you know."

"I pay my mam every week for my food and board, and washing and ironing my shirts and things."

"That's a good lad, I'm sure your mother's proud of you. A hard-working young man such as yourself, you're a credit to any mum," and she thought of Basil Boothroyd, and the 'things' she'd found in his wallet when she'd been tidying his room. Digusting!

He was becoming – no, he already was – quite depraved.

And careless. Not even his father should have found them. A single young man should not have the need to be taking such precautions – Oh, young people these days – and this very evening he could be on the rampage, frequenting a certain dance hall she'd heard, on very good authority, was little better than a brothel. Young woman were there flaunting themselves for one thing and one thing only – and not to dance!

"Are you and Basil… meeting up later?" and she purposely made it sound innocent.

He nodded.

"Then I hope the two of you have a very good evening. Basil needs… well, in the wrong company – and I do know the ways of the world, but if you're pals, then you'll look out for one other and neither of you get into any trouble."

He nodded again. It was easier that way.

The *Regent Hotel*, or the "whores' den" as it was otherwise known, had, that evening, an overpowering smell of disinfectant to hide the vomit that had been spewed over the bar and outside on the steps. The landlady, her hair tucked into a stocking top and held in place by two combs wore black, but she always wore black, summer or winter, night or morn. An outsize drooping bosom rested on a bulging waistline, the face bearing all the wrath of the Seven Beasts of the Apocalypse was devoid of all make-up as she hurled abuse at the man who managed to stagger back into the bar.

"No bloody service," she screamed.

He swayed precariously. Seconds later, now at the customer's side of the bar the woman in black began to forcefully remove him while the evening barman, a mincing little queen, stood watching as he stroked his fingernails. He smiled at the two young men as he suddenly came to life.

"Yes, gentlemen?"

"Two lagers."

Alan swallowed and suddenly felt queasy. "There's a bloody awful smell."

"Essence of poufter," and Basil nodded in the direction of the barman. "Watch yourself, he might fancy you."

"Then he'll be disappointed."

"It really does stink," Basil agreed, "so what d'you say we move after this one?"

"Find some other equally select establishment."

"Aye. And then – well – look out *Lyceum* Ballroom, here we come!"

The landlady returned, apparently no worse from her recent scuffle and the two men moved into the snug, where a couple of 'business girls' were hovering.

"D'you fancy owt with your lager?" Alan teased.

"When you've summatt this size between your legs," and he put his hand to his groin, "you can sell it, not buy it."

"Bragging. Self-praise no recommendation," yet that part of Basil Boothroyd's anatomy was no secret to the workforce of Boothroyd and Son, Decorators. The evening was warm, suit and tie uncomfortable, but if they were to descend on their usual Friday night hop and beat the other fellers to the best-looking girls, then they had to dress to impress.

Alan stared at the wallcovering, then nodding toward it said, "isn't it bloody awful."

"Absolutely, and the next pub we go to'll probably be the same."

"You'd think landlords would – " but there was a sudden commotion as a new crowd of punters descended on the *Regent* and, amid much laughter and merriment, fought their way into the snug.

"Bloody 'ell, it's like a football match. I wonder what's – " and then he stopped and called out, "Annie, good to see you."

Alan stared at the young woman, obviously the centre of attention. She was… well, if not one of the 'business girls' then certainly well-known to them.

"Who is she?" he muttered.

"It's Annie! She must have just come out. She's being doing nine months – she's the town's abortionist!"

"Eh?"

Basil nodded, then went on to explain, "she helps the girls out when they're in a spot of bother, you know. And Annie will… well, anything up to six months an' a breakfast, and she'll oblige."

"Really. And how come you know her?"

He smiled. "Alan, you pretend to know the ways of the world. Do I have to bloody spell it out? I got this bird up the duff, and Annie 'helped me out of what could have been a difficult situation' if you follow my drift. That's why I always wear a johnny now when I'm er… having fun, so it can't happen again."

"And I bought a packet this afternoon, just in case we get lucky tonight."

"Good lad. Now, I'll just go over and have a word with her. Say it's nice to see her back in circulation… We could even stay here for another half – and then – well… *Lyceum,* here we come!"

Chapter 5

"Wwweeelll" and she miawed like a cat that had stepped onto and sprung a baited mousetrap, "ah'm the eldest of nine children. I wor twenty when yer dad wor born. 'Ee wor 'baby o' family, an' it wor me as brought 'im up."

"Yes, aunt Muriel. Now, I must get started or I'll never – "

"An' yer aunt Ivy wor a poor affair. Eee, it's a wonder shu survived. Shu wor in bed fer weeks, until sumbody told mi mother 'er 'air wor sappin' all 'er strength. Lovely long curls she 'ad, till they cut 'em off. Then… well, she'd sore eyes till she 'ad 'er ears pierced. Gold, d'yer see. What's in golden eye ointment now, as folks use when they're got sore eyes."

"Fancy!"

"An' when women got 'a lump' as they described it, they'd poultice it wi' red clover. Yer see, in them days, things were different."

"Mmm," he agreed. Anything to keep the old dear quiet and out of his way.

"An' there wor no free 'Ealth Service," she nattered on, "no family allowance or owt. An' ah'd no time ter think abaht gettin' married when there were all that lot o' yer ter look after. Three sisters an' five brothers."

The yearly ritual of decorating for aunt Muriel never changed. She'd natter, natter, natter over anything and everything – and when you'd finished listening to her you were no wiser, for she'd said nothing.

There was just round the windows and the door to paper, an hour's work if she'd keep quiet and out of his way.

"Ooohhh, I can remember when we 'ad lovely Lincrusta – or wor it Anaglypta – 'alf way up 'wall? – an' we used ter varnish it every year."

"Oh aye?"

"But folk don't bother wi' things like that these days."

"No."

"An' we used ter 'ave lino wi' a pattern like proper polished wood floor. Ooohhh, it wor lovely."

"Them were the days, eh?"

"An' 'olidays? Well, goin' abroad then were no more na a week in 'Isle o' Man. Ah still pay inter a 'olidy club, though ah nivver go anywhere. Ah draw it aht every August, an' start payin;' in aggean 'end o' September, but these days folks get all over – an' bring back all sorts o' diseases."

"Yes, aunt."

"An' there's immigrants comin' thro far-off countries. Pollutin' atmosphere breathin' aht all that foreign stuff. Sumbody needs ter put a stop to it. I've been 'avin' reight funny 'eadaches an' all sorts – an' all ter do wi' this government. An all this bad weather wi' been 'avin'? It's since they tried gettin' ter mooin. Where's it all comin' from? Up there," and she pointed heavenward. "Space ships 'ave upset 'earth's crust, d'ter see,"

He nodded in agreement. It was easier, and looking round the room asked, "What do you do in the evenings then, aunt Muriel? Don't you fancy getting a tele?"

"Eee, no lad, yer see," and she held up his finger as a warning, "if you can see them on a screen, 'ow d'yer know they can't see you?"

"They'd have a lot of folk to watch."

"No, I like listenin' ter 'wireless. There's *Mrs Dale's Diary* on a mornin' an' *Workers' Playtime* when ah'm 'avin' me dinner. Then there's *Woman's 'Our* an 'in 'evenin' there's Wilfred Pickles *'Ave a Go.* 'Ee's local. Yer know. Thro 'Alifax."

"Oh, that's all right then, as long as you enjoy them." He had to get a move on, because when he'd finished listening to his aunt moan about anything and everything, he'd to finish papering her front room in time to get home for lunch and get changed before going to watch Huddersfield Town. Football matches were one of the highlights of his life, aunt Muriel's was cashing in on her 'It wor me as brought yer dad up, I wor twenty when 'ee wor born' by getting her decorating done for free.

On going through the turnstile his afternoon enthusiasm suddenly disappeared, and like a robot his eyes followed the moves of the players. He cheered along with those around him as the game progressed, but his mind was on other things. When the game was over he jumped into the van, deliberated, then decided to take the long way home.

He drove along Leeds Road toward Mirfield and Dewsbury, taking the right fork after passing the *Three Nuns.* A pub he'd never been in, it was the sort of place one drove past without stopping. Reaching Mirfield he took the right turn by the post office, past the railway station, went over the River Calder then turned right toward Liley Lane and Grange Moor.

Somewhere down one of the many winding lanes in Grange Moor was the pit known locally as 'Daniel's Day Oyle' where some of his uncles worked. Not deep enough to be regarded as a proper pit, but something more than mere outcropping.

The road swung to his right just past the church, on his left was the junior school, and just before reaching *New Inn* on his right was 'The Band Room' where the village band practised and kept their instruments. There was also a brass band in nearby Emley, also in Skelmanthorpe, and he seemed to imagine, in Lepton and Flockton.

Brass Bands and mining seemed to go together, alongside carnivals, and yearly Agricultural Shows, and – and he could smell it before he reached it – some few hundred yards further along at the cross road was Shuttle-Eye Colliery.

It had a spoil heap constantly emitting sulphur fumes day and night, and today was no exception, while perched on the horizon in the far distance was the winding gear to Fanny Main. A mile to his left was Nine Clogs Colliery, in the opposite direction Lepton Edge Pit. He seemed surrounded by them. It was as though they were beckoning – but they were going to be disappointed.

Yet he didn't seem to be able to escape from them, and imagining life underground and a world of utter blackness, suddenly remembered when as a little lad he'd gone to the pit manager's office with his mum to collect his dad's 'sick pay' as he was in bed with a bout of sciatica. He was shown round the lamp-room by old Charlie Eastwood, one of their neighbours, and was able to hold dad's pit lamp, for it was explained to him that every miner had his own.

"Are yer goin' ter work dahn 'pit wi' yer dad when yer grow up?"

"I'm going to be a doctor."

"By gum!"

As he drove toward Lepton Edge, Alan imagined how very different colliery workmates would be from the Basil Boothroyds of this world and (and he couldn't get it out of his mind) he thought again of the disgusting levels the two men had sunk to the previous night. Nor had he particularly enjoyed it, for 'to turn him on', his partner had to be quite a few years older than he was. Last night the girls at the *Lyceum* were young flighty things, but ready for 'fun'.

"Have you got a car?" was one of the first things his dancing partner asked.

He nodded.

"My name's Christine. That's my friend Jean who's dancing with your mate. We've seen the two of you here before."

"Mmm."

"What's your name then?"

"Alan."

"That's nice."

Nice? A name like Alan?

The music ended, the two couples drifted to the bar, and when the dancing finished, driving across the moors on the way to Holmfirth, Basil stopped the car, took the car rugs from the boot and spread them over the heather, as the real Friday night's fun began.

Before lust could be appeased and the girls transported to a world of ecstasy the men must perform amazing feats then change partners for a replay, and on the promise that they'd 'see them the following week' on reaching their destination, the girls were bundled out of the car, and the men laughed, admired and praised each other's stamina and prowess.

Some hundred yards from the Boothroyd home, Alan moved into the driving seat, on the off-chance that 'she who must be obeyed' might be lurking and see which of the two men was the driver – but that was the most innocent part of the night's activities.

The previous evening's escapades made him feel guilty, and decidedly dirty – but it had happened, and probably would the next time he and Basil descended on – well, not the *Lyceum* for the next few weeks, for his partner-in-crime had suggested a different future venue to give the girls the chance to get to know some other blokes.

The van took a turn to the left, before reaching Lepton Edge Colliery, then sticking out into the sky on a mound in front of the far horizon of the Pennine Range was Castle Hill.

The 'castle' was a tall tower from where, so his mum told him when he was much younger, a woman had jumped, hoping to end her life. But her billowing skirts had acted as a parachute and she glided down to safety and into the arms of her lover.

Now on the horizon was the Holme Moss television mast, and on the left of this and much nearer to him, the new mast had just been erected at Emley Moor, a village little heard of until this 'something' like a miniature Blackpool tower had been built.

He reached the top of Hob-Cote Bank and the row of two-up-one-down miners cottages, then turned down to the small cluster of houses in Thornlees Close, number seven, his parents home among them.

He glanced at the petrol gauge. He must put some more fuel in before getting to work on Monday. Four gallons and twenty Players for just under one pound if he called at one of the town garages, out in the sticks petrol was nearly twice the price. But his weekend roaming was nearly at an end.

Later that evening, with mum sat in front, his dad in the back comfortable on a pile of cushions, Boothroyd and Son, Decorators, headed toward the next village and the Working Men's Club.

Saturday night (after the twenty-six hand whist drive) was Bingo Night. Four and six for a line, sometimes as much as one pound ten shillings for a full house – there were fortunes to be made!

He sipped his draught Guinness, mam cuddled her sweet sherry, and dad seemed to keep disappearing to the gents, which was nothing more than a brick building about the size of a garage adjoining a semi-detached on a housing estate.

No cubicles, just a gully near the far wall. No hand-washing facilities, the illumination being from the street lamp at the side of the road. But the men usually went round the back of the building to relieve themselves in the grass, and in the winter, make yellow snow!

The sort of place Basil Boothroyd would have loved, being able to openly and unconcernedly flash his no-longer secret weapon to the miners, farmers and the like.

"An jackpot terneet stands at five pounds," a raucous, breathless voice wheezed, as the game was about to begin. Mam won a house. Alan had a second pint but decided against a third as mam kept nattering on about 'drinkin' an' drivin'. But at least he was free from any 'Basil Boothroyd' type temptation among the younger married women, who didn't know how to even innocently flirt. Mill girls with frizzy perms, middle aged women smelling of Devonshire Violets and old dears in twin sets and pearls and wearing skirts having what mam referred to as 'box pleats'.

That evening, indeed, the clientele was very restrained. No drunks, no fights, no amorous innuendoes, even the few fellers his age stayed in a clique and ignored him. They probably worked down the pit!

He'd be glad when he was home.

Chapter 6

He gave a second glance at the clothing he'd taken from the wardrobe drawer. He'd need to buy some new pairs of underpants, something eye-catching, but at the same time didn't want his mam to think he was 'goin' that way' as she politely described certain men, thought how she knew about such a thing was quite beyond him.

Then he'd need to buy some more pyjamas, not striped flannelette but something cool. Cotton, perhaps, or even something really sensuous – black silk! He'd need to take with him a pack of razors and shaving foam, after-shave lotion, deodorant, talc – oh, and he'd need to buy some new swimming trunks. He looked at the maroon woollen garment, and remembered when, several years ago after the pit-head baths had been built, his dad asking if he could borrow them to wear when he was taking a shower with his workmates?

In some things dad was very naïve, and it suddenly struck him, he'd never, not once seen his dad in the buff. This was a father and son 'bonding' that was yet to happen. But it might, it just 'might' if, at the end of working the same shift underground they were showering together. Better that he concentrated on his wardrobe, and clothes on, rather than off.

He might perhaps buy a couple of shirts, and some socks, and he opened the wardrobe door to examine his new sports jacket and flannels from John Colliers and his made-to-measure suit from Montague Burtons. The season's latest fashion colour for men, copper-bronze, he'd be OK, no need to buy – well, he'd several pairs of grey flannel trousers, jeans and the like. They were fine, nothing required in that department, but he'd need things like ties and cuff-links, then he again reminded himself, this holiday was for 'taking things off' rather than being dressed up and strutting about like a peacock!

But there were more pressing things than studying and debating on his holiday wardrobe, and on hearing the toilet flush knew it to be the signal that William Henry Beaumont had 'done the mornin's necessary' as he referred to such a thing, and that they could now have a couple of hours in the allotment.

There were broad beans to pick, the first of the crop of early potatoes to lift, spears of bindweed to tear out before they had a chance to establish themselves along with the other weekly tasks. Noah Jackson who had a greenhouse on the next plot had some tomatoes to barter for whatever took his fancy, mam needed some parsley for a sauce, and lettuce for the afternoon tea, when her sister Ada Martha would descend on them. A chapel organist, and not a woman to cross!

"An' what d'yer think o' 'er at number seventeen?"

"Eh?'

"Yer mean yer've not 'eard? Shu's three men stoppin' fer what shu politely calls 'Bed and Board.' Outcroppers workin' rahnd Emley Moor – an' all 'village knows what she's offerin'. The trollop! Eee, there's sum wickedness in 'world terday, even in little villages where we live. There's sin an' fornications wherever yer look."

William Henry crunched his stick of celery. When Ada Martha started there was no stopping her.

"Ah told 'em last week when we met at 'chapel fer 'Bright 'Our. Ah said, 'there'll be a reckonin' one o' these days. 'Vengeance is Mine, sayeth the Lord' – an' at the appointed time we'll all be judged. It's all in 'book o' Revelations – an' it's all comin' ter pass. This world's in a terrible state. Immoral acts, depravity," – and Alan thought again of his earlier Friday night antics on the moors above Holmfirth, and as though she could read the shame and guilt on his face aunt Ada Martha suddenly turned toward her nephew.

"Are yer keepin yersen pure?"

"Why, auntie, what d'you mean.?"

"Young men get… lecherous, lewd thoughts, an' sometimes they get out o' control."

"Oh?"

"Aye. I'm just sayin'!"

"Fancy." He struggled to keep a straight face, then felt somebody kick his shoe, and trying to put on an innocent expression asked "When they get… these thoughts, what should they do, auntie?"

"They need ter say 'Lord's Prayer, an' ask God ter guide 'em back ter 'paths o righteousness'.

"I'd better remember that."

Suddenly his aunt turned to her brother-in-law. " 'Ee needs guidance! 'Ee could be lost fer ever. Drowned in a sea o' shame an' depravity. Oh, the wickedness o' men!"

"Get thee tea, an' dooant talk so damned silly," Gladys Beaumont tried to end the topic of conversation of which her sister was so very fluent.

"Well, ahm just sayin'."

"Tha's gettin' as bad as our Rhoda."

"Nay, shu's nobbut eleven pence ter 'shillin' these days. Goin' ter 'Spiritualist church, an' spirit-rappin' sessions 'ave driven 'er potty. She tells folks as'll listen to 'er that shu's in daily communication wi' Saint Bernadette, no less – an' between 'em they're 'goin' ter save the world. Shu'll end up in Storthes 'All loony bin. Shu's daft as they cum!"

"Yer didn't owt ter talk like that abaht ah Rhoda."

"It's true. True as ah'm sittin' 'ere,"

"Well," and Alan steered himself from what could develop into a family argument, "I need to get the van washed before tomorrow morning. I'll attend to it now."

"An' will it be Blackpool next weekend?" aunt Ada Martha enquired of her nephew before he could disappear.

"Er… oh yes," he lied.

"Fer two weeks?"

He nodded, gulping down the rest of his meal, while aunt Ada Martha continued nattering on about Spiritualism and the state of the world, as he filled a bucket at the sink he once thought about the holiday and the lies he was having to tell. Then, on a totally different plain, imagined life in Germany or at an air force base in… well, anywhere away from daft old aunts ready for the loony bin.

It could be worth it – being away from home suddenly had distinct advantages!

Chapter 7

Suitcases packed and by the door, he swallowed a quick breakfast before saying a hasty farewell to mum and dad, then headed to the bus stop. There were other villagers waiting with dubious bits of luggage and bags – probably all going to Blackpool and staying in back street boarding houses, and they would every day casually bump into each other in R.H.O. Hills or on the pleasure beach. At the end of the holiday the men would have blistered foreheads, their wives sore sunburnt arms, but Wakes Weeks were a thing they looked forward to, and of their return home the women would join another 'holiday club' to help pay for the following year's two weeks in Blackpool.

Alan kept his distance from the Johnsons who lived only a few doors away. Eva Johnson was an evil old cow at the best of times, and she was giving him somewhat suspicious looks, as though she knew 'something' was afoot. But she couldn't, he was imagining it. Suddenly, in the distance he could see a smudge, blue and white, slowly app-roaching. The Huddersfield bus. In less than thirty minutes – but every second was an eternity, it would reach its destination. He kept his suitcases close to him and sat away from those he knew. Intimate conversations were the last thing he wanted.

The morning transport to holiday paradise gathered momentum, the sun was breaking through, and he was more than a little bit 'queasy' when he thought of what was afoot. The bus approached the main Huddersfield Wakefield road then turned left. The next village would be Lepton, and he mentally tried counting the nearby villages ending with the suffix '-ton'. There was Lepton, Dalton, Kirkheaton, Hopton, Flockton, Kirkburton, Bretton, and toward Wakefield was Overton, toward Barnsley was Darton. Someone had told him that in the middle ages 'ton' meant town – it must have been a very busy part of Yorkshire.

He stared down at his shoes. Anything, anything to take his mind off what was about to – or might not, as the case may be, happen on his reaching his destination.

He purposely held back until the locals, anxious to arrive at the railway station or Cross Church Street which was where the holiday coaches were waiting were out of sight and on their way. He was to head in the opposite direction when it was safe to do so without his being noticed. Two minutes later he furtively glanced over his shoulder before turning into Byram Street and saw, some fifty yards away the apple green Baby Austin. As he approached, the driver turned down her window and in mock severity greeted him. "Good morning, Mr Hunter."

"And good morning to you, Mrs Hunter," he acknowledged her greeting, then the two of them burst out laughing.

"We need to get away quick, before anybody sees us", and he gave yet another look over his shoulder.

"Mmm, I agree. Get your suitcases on the back seat, and you can drive, I'll be the passenger. Of course, we don't need to arrive for hours yet, perhaps early evening if it's been a lunch time wedding and reception. We could even make a detour and have a couple of hours looking round York and going somewhere for a meal.

"Sounds good."

"And I have here, for when we do descend on the hotel, some confetti to casually sprinkle over ourselves."

"Rosemary, you think of everything," and as he took the wheel he began to think… of his employer and his wife, and his best mate, even the possible wrath of his own parents if this holiday should in any way become public knowledge. What he and Rosemary Boothroyd were embarking upon was exciting – but it was also dangerous!

Mr And Mrs Hunter? If you'd like to sign the visitors book, you're on the first floor overlooking the sea, and with a private bathroom. It's been a lovely day, hasn't it."

Rosemary Boothroyd, looking like a demure virgin nodded, and her eyes went to her partner. "A perfect day. Absolutely perfect." And she touched the plain gold ring on the third finger of her left hand.

"…And Amy will show you to your room. If you need anything… anything at all, please don't hesitate to ask. We've been in this business for many years and we like our guests to feel welcome and comfortable."

As Alan leaned forward to sign his name sprinklings of confetti as earlier arranged fell from his pocket. The receptionist smiled, her silence spoke volumes.

"We could have dinner here, or we could…"

"Yes?"

"No, not that. I mean, meander into the town centre and find somewhere to eat."

"But Mrs Hunter," Alan teased, "this is our wedding night. Let's dine in style in the hotel restaurant. We'll probably get looked after and fussed over much more than is we went for fish and chips on the seafront."

"More than likely. Do you think we've fooled them?"

"Absolutely. Completely. The old dear on reception will probably feel she should take you to one side to have a 'motherly' talk to you, while her husband will tell me to be 'gentle' with you."

"Heaven help us. What have we started?"

"Our fortnight's honeymoon. Now, Mrs Hunter, are you going to look the other way while I change into something more comfortable?"

"I'd rather get a surprise."

"That'll come later, never fear," and he thought of his usual routine.

He'd perfected it to a fine art. Tonight would be no exception.

The meal was leasurely and relaxed. The food was first-rate, as was the way in which it was served. Then there were drinks in the bar, with the waiter giving them knowing looks. Probably the entire staff and the other guests knew that this young couple, Mr and Mrs Hunter, had been married earlier that day, and were having a sip of 'Dutch courage' before the bride gave herself to her new husband, who would perform what was expected of him in a most gentlemanly way.

An elderly couple smiled at them on every possible occasion. She was wrinkled and permed dressed in dark blue trimmed with white lace, he'd a moustache he was doing his best to control by stroking it, as he thought about 'stroking' other things.

Rosemary glanced at her watch. "Do you think we should be making a move?"

"Mmm. When we've finished our drink, And he leaned across the table and took her hand. "Mrs Hunter?"

"Yes?"

"I love you very much." He spoke loud for the others to hear. "You've made me the happiest man in the world."

She lowered her head to suppress her mirth, then holding aloft her left hand so all could see the ring on her finger she replied "Thank you, Mr Hunter. And now, let's get to bed."

He was used to what would undoubtedly follow, for so many, many times had he played this card.

He purposely fumbled with his shoe laces, then removed his tie and carefully folded it, and hung it with his shirt over the back of a chair. He searched through his suitcase for the bag containing his toiletries, "I… er… ought to get shaved… unless you need to…"

She shook her head, then slipped out of her clothes, and Alan turned his gaze to the bra now on the bedroom floor.

"Well… I'll… er… only be a few minutes."

"Right, Mr Hunter. I'll just pull the sheets down and… which side of the bed would you like?"

He just stared, as would an innocent three-year- old, and finally shrugged his shoulders.

"Well, go and get shaved then," she took command, "and then you'd better…"

"Rosemary, there's something I must tell you."

"Later. When you're next to me."

"Yes, but you see… I haven't…"

"Brought any toothpaste? Well, I have. Use mine."

He looked round in desperation… any second now, but he'd get shaved and perform anything else that was necessary first. 'Things' had to be clean, and he might need to… anyway, he'd get shaved first.

After what seemed an eternity to both occupants of the first floor room with a view overlooking the sea Alan, wearing nothing more than his underpants, modestly turned down the sheets on his side of the bed and effortlessly slid close to his employer's daughter.

If Constance Boothroyd ever found out, or worse still, Rosemary's twin brother Basil, then all hell would be let loose. He tried to get comfortable and wanted to break wind, but knew he mustn't.

A voice interrupted his thoughts.

"Alan."

"Mmm?"

"Alan, is everything all right?"

"Yes, why do you ask?"

"Well, you're gone sort of 'quiet', and – "

"And I'm frightened I'm going to be such a let-down. You see… I've never…"

"Eh?"

"You know. Oh, I've had lots of girlfriends, and done lots of boasting to my mates… but I've never… done *that.*"

"You mean…" and she stared in near disbelief, "you've never made love to anyone?"

He shook his head. "Rosemary, you should have come away on holiday with some feller who… oh, I don't know how to put it politely, but someone who knows what it's all about, this… sex thing."

"But *I* know." And her arms went out to him. "Alan, there has to be a first time for everything – and for everybody."

"But if I've never… I might not be doing it right."

"Relax," and loving arms went round the self-confessed virgin. "You're going to have what I hope will be the most wonderful experience of your life. And we have all night… no, two whole weeks together. We don't want to rush things, or have all our passions spent in just a few minutes, do we?"

"No…"

"Now," and Rosemary took command, "I think we should remove your underpants, and then…"

"Yes…?"

"We can become better acquainted," she whispered, drawing his hand to her breast.

"A splendid suggestion, Mrs Hunter. And I've been reliably informed that during lovemaking, a gentleman takes his body-weight on his elbows, so to speak."

"Then you must when… but first… Mr Hunter, we have to explore," and a hand took his and placed it on a most intimate part of her anatomy. "And we have all the time in the world… to explore… caress, and… my Alan." She flattered him, "you really are a big boy where it matters."

He sighed with pleasure. This holiday could be something to remember for many years to come.

Chapter 8

"It's sort of… in a time warp, if you follow my meaning," and he stared beyond the statue of Captain Cook and the arched whale bones visible from their bedroom window reaching toward the sky like giant elephant tusks, and behind them blue and so-calm sea.

"Mmm," Rosemary agreed, "Certainly different from, say, Blackpool's Golden Mile."

"And that's where all the locals from where I live will be for the next fortnight, well, the rest of this week, certainly. Some families can only afford a week away at best."

"And so… what do you fancy doing today?"

He took her into his arms. "Spending it in bed with you, where we can," and his hands were beginning to stray, "explore each others' naughty bits. Lots of foreplay before we get down to the real business."

"Mr Hunter," she replied in pretended shocked tones.

"Oh, Mrs Hunter, I do so love this game we're playing."

"But when the holiday's over and we're back at work, what's going to happen?"

"Well, I've not really thought about it. We can't… we must keep it a secret or your dad'll kick me out, but not before Basil punches the living daylights out of me, if he thinks I've seduced and ruined his twin sister."

And he thought of the things he and Basil Boothroyd had done on their Friday night escapades, and here he was with his partner in crime's twin sister pretending that sex was something new to him. He turned to her, a pleading look on his face. "We can keep it our secret, can't we?"

She nodded. It was easier than a confrontation with her mother who was planning her marrying someone far above a mere 'Painter and Decorator'.

"Shall we go down into the town and go over the bridge to look at the shops on Church Street. There'll be jewellers selling Whitby jet rings and brooches, and there's the old Town Hall and lots of little alleyways They're very quaint. Or we could even climb the hundred and ninety-nine steps up to the abbey."

She stared. "As many as that?"

"So I believe," then he added, "but we don't have to count them. And when we get to the top we can always stare at the headstones in the churchyard and start asking where Dracula is buried."

"Don't you dare."

"It's all right, I'm only joking."

"Right, that's settled. And tomorrow…" and Rosemary took command, "we might journey further up the coast. There's lots of little fishing villages. Runswick, Staithes – and we could even call at Saltburn, and go up as far as Redcar, if you like."

"Sounds good."

"If we were to go in the opposite direction toward Ravenscar and eventually Scarborough we might…"

"Bump into some holiday-makers who know us," he finished her sentence, and shook his head. "No." he took her in his arms, "I'm a very lucky feller, Rosemary. I'd like to shout it to the world, but it's you I'm thinking about. Let's go where we'll not be recognised."

It was a day of visiting the tiny fishing villages Rosemary had earlier described. They sampled the delights of Sandsend, then Kettleness, Runswick, Port Mulgrave and then the fishing village of Staithes.

As they made their way down the cobbled street, women that he took to be fishermen's wives stood at their doorways, watching. In wrap-around pinnies, their arms folded, they stared at these strangers defiantly.

They passed a couple of village shops, then, as the road swung to the right, on their left there was an alleyway leading to a bridge, and the lifeboat station. There were further alleyways looking secret and foreboding, reminding Alan of some he'd seen in Whitby. Then the road led to yet another pub, the *Cod and Lobster*, which seemed to jut out into the sea. A further hundred yards the road met the cliff and came to an end.

“Staithes must a very thirsty place,” Alan commented, “to have a Working Mens’ at the top of the village, then the Black Lion, the Royal George, and…”

“And several places of worship, they must be a very religious and God-fearing community,” Roosemary observed. “We’ve passed… let’s see… a church before the car park, then one, or was it two chapels? And there to our right, there’s Saint Peters.”

“All that in a village little more than a cobbled street with yards and alleyways.”

“Yet at the beginning of century the village was sort of ‘adopted’ by a colony of artists who became known as the Staithes Group, Several of them came from the West Riding. There was Mark Senior from Dewsbury. Mother has one of his paintings, an ‘original’ of course that she boasts about on every possible occasion. Then there was Henry Hill, from Halifax, Owen Bowen from Leeds and several others.”

“And your mum has painting by them as well?”

“No, just a couple. But the way she can go on about them, you’d think they were worth millions.”

“I don’t suppose there’ll be any for sale in Whitby, that we could take her as a sort of ‘holiday present’.”

“Fortunately, no. Besides, if she knew I’d been holidaying in this area, then she would be curious as to what I’d been up to. Better she imagines I’ve gone abroad for a fortnight.”

He smiled. “You think of everything, Mrs Hunter.”

Alan stared at the waves breaking on the shore, then they slowly retraced their steps, but on reaching the sharp bend in the street they turned down the alleyway toward the bridge. There were lobster-pots piled up like giant rat cages, sou’westered fishermen about their business by their moored fishing cobles, and, Alan reasoned, in this obviously close-knit community men must rely on their fellow men as did the miners in the West Riding.

At low tide the beck exposed its secrets. Fish innards, old ropes, buckets of kitchen waste – just about anything and everything. Alan took a long look. “Let’s move!”

Further along the coastal road they called at a pub for lunch before heading toward Saltburn, which, they decided was 'more than a village' but not quite a town before finally arriving at the destination, Redcar, which to Alan was somewhat of a disappointment. Certainly, he felt, not a place for a fortnight's holiday. No, Whitby had been an altogether superior choice.

"Let's get back to Whitby."

"So soon? But we've only nicely arrived."

"But, Mrs Hunter, I have an irresistible urge to make love to you. Something far more beautiful than 'sex'." And he put his arms around her. "Oh, Mrs Hunter, you're creating a terrible tightening in the trouser department.'

"So I can see."

"Well then?"

"We'd better head toward the car."

"We might even find somewhere quiet on the way back." And he looked hopeful. For soon, in a few days, it might all be over.

Chapter 9

"Are yer all reight, lad?" the voice at the end of the phone enquired.

"Mmm, I'm fine."

It was eight-thirty Sunday evening, the appointed day and time when Alan had promised to ring the public phone box at the top of the village to assure his waiting parents that all was well.

""Enjoyin' yer 'oliday?" his mum had commandeered the handpiece.

"Yes. Having a lovely time."

"Look after yersen – yer nooan gettin' blistered wi' sunburn, are yer. Put plenty calamine lotion on yer arms' ."

"No, no I'm O.K., really," and he rubbed up against the woman next to him. Mrs Hunter was wearing the most seductive perfume, and her fingers were exploring, exciting him. He smiled as hands became more searching, his trousers zip was being undone, then his father's voice brought him back to reality. "We'll see yer Sat'day afternooin, an' then cum Sunday we've company fer afternooin teea."

"Oh, aunt and uncle…"

"No. 'Pickersgills. An' Mavis is comin' wi' 'em."

Later that night, their passions spent but still in each other's arms, Alan thought about the return to 'normality' – but much more pressing, the Sunday afternoon with the Pickersgills. It had the beginnings of something akin to a medieval marriage arranged between the aristocracy, only the participants would be a mill girl and a painter and decorator. His mum would be going to a great deal of trouble, washing windows and painstakingly vacuuming carpets and the three piece suite, making sure the bathroom was spick and span, even the bedrooms tidy for she'd want to show mother and daughter what a clean household they'd come to – and it was all going to be for nothing.

Of course, he could always drop the bombshell by casually mentioning the young woman he'd just been on holiday with. Older than he was, more experienced than some plain mill girl with a spotty complexion and permanently smelling of her trade. One couldn't get rid of the smell of mill – but he supposed he himself moved in an odour of paint and distemper.

Oh, they'd make a wonderful couple – you'd smell them a mile off!

"Are you all right?" his bed-mate disturbed his thoughts.

"Mmm. I'm just sort of thinking… about when the holiday's over."

"When in the words of the song 'You must return to your world, I must go back to mine'".

"Do we have to?"

"Alan, this is something we need to discuss in great detail. We have to be certain, both of us, before we can go public, so to speak. I'm several years older than you. If it were the other way round then it wouldn't matter so much – and there are our families to consider."

"You mean, your mum's planned something more posh than – "

"No, I'm not interested in what she's planned, that doesn't come into it."

"But don't you see, I'm in love with you."

"Eh?"

"Well, don't sound so surprised. I love you! There, I've said it again. I love you. I love you." He drew her closer. "I know that at the outset this was supposed to be… well, just a holiday fling. I accept that you're several years older than me, but I'm not interested in silly young lasses my age. I also know your mum. And for the boss's daughter to marry one of his workmen isn't really the thing – and know that soon… any day now I could be starting National Service and be away for a couple of years and that the immediate future looks grim – but I still love you."

"Alan," she tried to calm his emotions, "what you're saying, even after the things we've been getting up to still come as a surprise. We need time to think about this carefully."

"You mean, you don't feel as I do?"

"I don't mean that at all. I'm thinking about you now. When the weekend comes we'll be leaving Whitby and… oh, I don't know. We have to have a long think about what we're going to do. But right now, Mr Hunter, every second is important," and Alan Beaumont kissed her gently, and words became no longer necessary.

Actions said it all.

Chapter 10

Cliftonville, Constance Boothroyd had already decided, would be favoured the following year by herself and her husband.

Blackpool, Scarborough, Skegness and the like were perhaps suitable for the working classes but the owner and the driving force of Boothroyd and Son deserved something better.

The hotel and meals had been superb, and was somewhere she could personally recommend to those with taste and discernment, and as she roamed through the strangely quiet house her thoughts went to her children. Rosemary on holiday with 'a friend', and Constance (though she should not even think such things) hoped that the 'friend' might be a young solicitor or something of that ilk, and that on their return he would ask for her hand in marriage.

A spring wedding?

Wonderful! But it would need careful planning, and she would supervise the arrangements herself. And regarding her son, Basil? Well, she trembled to think. Depravities, drunken orgies – he could even be behind bars. Oh no, his antics were to disgusting to even contemplate. One day there would come a reckoning.

But there were now more important matters. St. Peter's had, as in previous years, invited her to be the soloist for their Harvest Festival, and she would be singing for both afternoon and evening services. Probably *Let the Bright Seraphim* and *My Heart ever Faithful* and… something from Handel's *Messiah*. Rosemary, on her return, would be her accompanist for rehearsing, and Constance again prided herself on encouraging her daughter's love for music, and she would be home in a couple of days, and might perhaps want to confide to the mother a big secret.

That she was in love… with… the only son of a Lord! She thought of rambling stately homes and a long gallery (every stately home had one) with paintings by Titian, Venetian scenes by Canaletto, portraits and landscapes by Constable – oh, it was all becoming far too much for her to comprehend

Boothroyds really would be climbing the social ladder, with a daughter who would upon her marriage be Lady… well, whatever.

Just the thought of it set her senses racing. She'd need to go to London for some new clothes.

Or Paris!

Glad to be away from his ever-nagging wife, the owner of Boothroyds sought refuge in his office (even though it was still Holiday Fortnight). He felt a glow of inner satisfaction as he contemplated the ever-growing workload. When annual holidays were over they would need to take on extra staff, certainly 'casual workers' if the tenders submitted for the Town Hall were successful.

Satisfied clients made for even more satisfied clients, and the Auctioneer and Valuer two streets away (and who had recently become a Lodge Member) was taking very seriously the idea the 'Lodge Members help one another' by persuading all those people who had been left a property and wanted to put it on the market that "every ten pounds spent on painting and decorating could put a hundred on the asking price" – and then suggest a "very reputable and long-established firm of Decorators just round the corner."

By way of return, Constance Boothroyd would be seen scrutinising her catalogue and examining goods on 'view days' prior to the Antique and Collectors auctions held regularly, or when there was an auction of builders materials and the like then Basil (and more often than not) work colleague Alan Beaumont would look at the goods on offer. Clarence Woodhouse on recognising them would come forward, fingers would go to his temples to adjust his toupee and whatever they were examining would assure them "it's come from a very good family."

Basil and Alan on leaving the saleroom would mimic, And if they saw a dog doing something on the pavement for passer's by to walk in, or some grossly overweight individual wobbling out of a shop doorway, one would turn to the other and excuse them by saying "It comes from a very good family" before adjusting toupees and bursting out laughing.

But the two lads were more than best of pals, they were like brothers, and it was, he reasoned, quite likely that they'd gone on holiday together to somewhere like Butlins, and were having the time of their lives. He doubted that they would be holidaying abroad, for the South of France seemed more Constance than Basil. His thoughts turned to his friend Alan. He was a good lad, and when he did go into the army or wherever, Boothroyds would miss him, and not just because he was the firm's official driver, but because, being a pal, he was helping to keep Basil out of trouble. He thought of his own mis-spent youth, and the love-child he'd fathered, but that was, and he paused to mentally calculate, thirty five, thirty six years ago. It was a heavy, guilty secret – and it would need to remain so, for if Constance was to get even the slightest inkling of this illegitimate offspring resulting from a casual fling, then all hell would be let loose.

Sometimes when he looked at the 'Court in Brief' column of the local paper, a 'certain' name appeared. He was regularly in front of the magistrates, for being drunk and disorderly, petty theft, rent arrears and various driving offences. He was, of course, unemployed, and though unmarried lived with some woman he'd had five children to. Oh, if Constance ever – no, it would be too terrible to even contemplate!

"Now then, Mr Hunter – it's the last time I must call you this – where in Huddersfield should we part company?"

"Somewhere quiet. Perhaps by the library."

"And then... we shall see each other first thing Monday morning, and you'll be Alan Beaumont, Painter and Decorator, working for Boothroyds, and I shall be Rosemary Boothroyd, office girl and the boss's daughter."

"Rosemary, you're not in any way regretting what we've done, are you?"

She shook her head. "No."

"Good. And I'll say it now, because I realise that when we get to work I can't – I love you, and I hope these last two weeks will be the start of what will be our lifetime together."

"Alan, you – "

"Look, two years National Service will soon pass, and if after that time… you know, I'll still feel the same as I do now."

"Well, Mr Hunter, you've said your piece, so we must wait and see what transpires."

The traffic lights changed to green, Alan signalled and turned left, brought the Baby Austin to a halt and removed his suitcases.

Chapter 11

"Eee, coom in, lad."

He left his suitcases by the door as he entered a kitchen now scupulously clean and tidy.

"Yer mam 'as bin throng."

"So I see. She's even polished the Singer sewing machine."

"Oh aye. An' done 'treadle wi' black-leead, same she used ter do 'fireside wi'. Oh, an' shu's gooan ter 'Uddersfield ter get soom 'salad tomaters' as shu calls 'em. And shu's callin' at that butchers next ter 'market 'all ter get a big pooak pie. Onyroad, did yer 'ave a good 'oliday?"

"Mmm. Very nice."

"An' ah can see as yer've getten sunburnt."

"Oh yes."

"Nah then, dooant go an' upset owt in 'front room, 'cos it's all lookin' posh, an' yer mun put yer stuff away when yer empty yer suitcases."

"Yes." He looked again at the spick-and-span kitchen. It didn't seem like the home he'd left earlier. There was nothing, absolutely nothing out of place.

"Oh, an' ah think Mavis is lookin' for'ard ter meetin' yer."

"Oh."

But before the conversation could get any further, Alan knew that he must get out of the house. The garden? Up to the allotment? Anywhere so long as he was away from the conversation that would be certain to follow .

"I'll go and say 'Hallo' to aunt Muriel, and see how the room looks now she'll have all the ornaments back in place, and I'll take her a stick of rock."

"Aye, shu'll like that."

Suitcases went upstairs and were temporarily shoved under the bed after the presents had been removed. The two-mile walk to aunt Muriel's would give him time to think.

He needed both.

Time, certainly!

"Coom an' look what a've gooan an' bought."

She stood with a childish, imbecilic look on her face then led him up the stairs, and as an afterthought added, "ah've spent all mi' 'oliday club money on it, an' a bit more besides."

"On what?" a puzzled nephew enquired.

"It's in 'spare bedroom," she ignored his question, then, on opening the door announced, "It's me coffin!"

"Eh?"

"Fer when ah go up ter 'Eaven. Ah'm gettin' all 'arrangements made, an' ah've bought a lovely white nightdress wi' fergetmenots on it ter be laid aht in. A've chosen mi' funeral 'ymns an' 'bible readin's, an' look what it says on' lid. Muriel Beaumont. Born a virgin, died a virgin."

"It sounds as though you've got it all planned out." Alan stared in awe as she continued, "An' ah'm goin' ter paint bunches o' flowers all 'way rahnd, an tie big bows o' red ribbon on brass 'andles. What d'yer think?"

"Well, it'll be different."

"When I wor young ah wanted ter be a nun – but ah'd all 'family ter look after, bein' eldest. Oh, an' ah've put labels on all mi stuff sayin who's ter 'ave what. Ah'm goin'ter leave yer dad yer grandad's gold watch an' chain."

"He'll… appreciate that."

"An it's real gold. Twenty two carat. A 'alf 'unter."

"An' yer aunt Martha'll playin' organ. 'Andel's *Largo,* cos shu can manage that withaht 'ittin 'ter many wrong notes. Yer sud 'ear 'er sum Sundays.' Shu could be playin' owt. Then, when mi coffin's brought dahn ter 'front there'll be 'first 'ymn an' a bible readin' then after 'prayer, an' – would yer like ter read twenty-third psalm?"

"But I might not be here. No, I could be on some ship in the middle of the ocean, or even at some army training camp in Germany. I could be getting my call-up papers any day now."

"But yer goin' dahn 'pit wi' yer dad. 'Ee wor tellin' me all abaht it nobbut last week. It's all arranged."

"Eh?"

"Aye. Didn't yer know?"

"Well, I didn't until now."

"Nah, dooant let on. Ah dooant want 'im ter think ah've been tellin' tales an' tryin' ter cause bother, but – "

"Don't worry aunt Muriel, you haven't said a word." He took a deep breath and looked at his watch. "My, I didn't know it was so late, I must be moving. Enjoy your stick of rock."

"Oh ah will lad, nivver fear."

He had to get away. Things were getting too much.

It was a Saturday night of mum fussing over him, and his father trying not to get under her feet as she searched for, and ruthlessly attacked particles of dust that defiantly dared to take up residence. Alan thought of the previous evening he and Rosemary had spent making love… and so wanted to… well, not say what had actually taken place, but at least, tell them about his feelings toward Rosemary Boothroyd. But it was not the right moment for such revelations.

He deliberated. Should he go into town or ask dad if he fancied a drink? This way they could both escape from the cleaning orgy and enjoy a couple of pints in the Red Lion or the Working Mens'.

His father was reading his thoughts. "Ah dooant s'pose as we've ony bottles o' Guinness in 'top cupboard?"

The newly permed hair-do shook her head.

"Ah weel, it wor just a thought."

"Let's go for a drink," Alan was quick to grab the opportunity, "what d'you say, dad?"

"Go on, 'pair o' yer. Ah't thro under mi feet."

On their way to the Working Men's they passed the public phone box, and Alan was tempted… but if her mother or father picked up the receiver, then how could he make an excuse for wanting to have a conversation with their daughter? If it were Basil he could suggest a meet-up the following evening. But if it were Rosemary herself, then she could be extremely annoyed with his impertinence and insistence. She might not see it as an uncontrollable love urge, more of a bloody nuisance. His father's voice interrupted his thoughts. "Shu really is lookin' for'ard ter meetin' up wi' yer."

"Er, you mean – "

"Why, Mavis. Who else?"

He remained silent, it was much safer. But he couldn't help thinking, if the situation was in reverse, and Rosemary was being forced to meet some man her parents were hoping she'd marry, how would he feel? Cheated? Second best? Having been taken for ride. Used, only to be dumped if someone better came along. No, Rosemary must never find out what his parents were planning – nor that he was having to go along with their schemes.

Even after two bottles of Newcastle Brown the situation seemed little better. Hovering in his mind was an image of a lanky haired, straight-up-and-down figure of the fifteen-year-old, which was as he remembered Mavis Pickersgill to be, and both sets of parents were thinking of a live-happy-ever-after wedding – he might even forget the army or the navy – twenty-five years in the Foreign Legion seemed suddenly very desirable.

"Coom on in, 'missis is expectin' yer," and William Henry Beaumont smiled as he held open the door to allow the guests entrance.

"This is Rhoda." Frank Pickersgill appologised for the shapeless, grossly overweight woman dressed in a grey costume and ridiculous hat who was searching through her handbag. The handkerchief was located, the woman blew her nose then announced, "Ah'm pleased ter make yer acquaintance."

"An' this must be Mavis. Cum in, luv, mek yerselves at 'ome. T'wife's in 'front – " and then a door opened. "No, shu's 'ere. Gladys, meet us company."

Hovering in the background were a young man and woman, the reason for this meeting of the two families. One lovesick for his boss's daughter, the other believing that this was the 'official' introduction to her husband-to-be. She was, as Alan vaguely remembered, plain!

Nondescript hair style, and a face devoid of any make-up. She wore a maroon cardigan over a pale green dress, and Alan suddenly remembered a film he'd seen where Henry VIII first met Anne of Cleves. Holbein had portrayed her as a very beautiful woman, but in reality she was…

" 'Allo Alan."

…like Mavis Pickergill.

"Hallo."

"It's a long time since we were at school together."

"Mmm."

"D'yer want a cup o' tea affore we sit dahn ter us meal proper?"

"Aye,'" William Henry answered for the assembled company, "that'd be grand."

"Ah'll just go put 'kettle on then,"and totally unaware of the can of worms she was opening, she asked, "Are yer keepin' well, Rhoda?"

"Better na ah wor six month back, bur ah'm still gettin' palpitations an' 'problems', d'yer see. An' 'eadaches? Ooohhh, summatt terrible!"

"Are yer takin' owt?"

"Well, ah go ter 'Uddersfield once a month ter see sumbody, an' get sum 'erbs or a bottle o' summatt ter 'elp me relax."

"Shu's in 'change, d'yer see," Frank Pickersgill explained his wife's condition, "an' shu's been ter quacks all over 'West Ridin' ter find sumbody as could cure 'er."

"There's one wi' a magic glass, d'yer know," the grey costumed figure announced, "an' 'ee puts it on yer for'eead then looks into it, an' 'ee can see straight through yer, ter see what's wrong. Could be yer liver, yer 'eart, or yer could 'ave problems," and she gave a cough, "dahn there. But 'ee can see whats wrong an' gi'e yer summatt as'll help put things reight."

"An' it costs, an' all, 'avin' glass on yer 'eead," her husband dared to speak, but she fixed him with a look, and he knew not to elaborate on his earlier statement.

“Did yer ’ave a nice ’oliday, Alan?” Rhoda Pickersgill changed the subject.

“Mmm. Very nice.”

“We went to Blackpool last year an’ I ’ad a ride on ’Big Dipper, an’ when I got off I were sick all over front o’ mi dress,” Mavis boasted. “Oohhh, ah wor poorly. Candy floss an’ fish an’ chips all came back,” and Alan thought of the trifle his mum had made with the wobbly custard, and no longer felt hungry. Throughout the meal the subjects seemed to alternate between working on the coalface and the various herbalists and ‘quack doctors’ in the West Riding. Dewsbury, Huddersfield, Wakefield, Pudsey, Birstall… every town seemed to have one, but – and Rhoda Pickersgill spoke with good authority – only one had a ‘magic glass’.

Although vague references were made regarding ‘opportunities’ for young men at the local pit, they were no more than that, then Frank Pickersgill suddenly switched the conversation be asking, “ ’Eard owt yer abaht goin’ in ’army?”

“Well,” and Alan grabbed the opportunity, ”call-up papers could be arriving any day. And there’ll be a medical of course, and perhaps… oh, I don’t know how it works exactly, but I might go in the Navy, if I get the choice. You know the song ‘All the nice girls love a sailor.’ It could be fun, having lots of lasses touching your collar for luck.”

“We dooant want ony o’ that sort o’ talk.”

“But dad, you know National Service is something that can’t be avoided, unless I fail the medical by having some serious, life-threatening illness, which I haven’t. I’m remarkable fit.” He thought again of the antics of the previous fortnight. Rosemary Boothroyd could vouch for his stamina.

“Oh aye.” Frank Pickergill complimented him, “yer look a big strong lad. What d’yer do in yer spare time, then?”

Alan considered. “Help dad in the garden. Go out for a drink with my mates. I go swimming twice a week… and… you know…”

“Oh aye. Ah get yer drift.”

“And I go dancing Friday nights. Sometimes to the Mecca at Leeds of Bradford… depends,” and he thought about the last time he and

Basil had been to the *Lyceum* in Huddersfield, and the antics on the way to Holmfirth.

Oh, if Basil knew about his holiday with his twin sister, then it really would hit the fan.

"An' what do you do in yer spare time, Mavis?" Alan's father enquired.

"I like knittin'. Scarves and gloves – oh, an' ah knitted a pullover fer me dad."

"That'll keep 'im warm. An' there yer are, d'yer see," and he turned to his son, "ask Mavis nice, like, an' shu might knit you summatt as'll keep yer warm."

"To wear in the Navy? That'd go down well."

"Are yer serious abaht goin' in 'Navy?" And Rhoda Pickersgill wiped her forehead. "All that watter, makes me poorly just thinkin' abaht it."

"No, it's only summatt ter talk abaht," his father tried to calm the situation. "We know where 'ee'll and up," and he crunched on his stick of celery, bringing to topic to a sudden end.

"An' yer mun call on us next Sat'day afternooin. It's Shatt Fair weekend."

"Eee, that'll be grand."

"We've nooann been ter Skelmanthorpe Fair fer… oh, three or four year, 'ave we, William."

The local village fairs followed a strict time pattern. First, in early May was Emley Fair, followed by Kirkheaton, or as it was known locally, 'Yetton Rant'. Then there was Kirkburton, Honley Feast (though there was no fairground, as such), next was Skelmanthorpe, or Shatt Fair, and last of all, when the nights were drawing in, Flockton Fair. At each venue would be the usual penny slot-machines, rolling penny stalls, swing boats, rides on the waltzer, where men with

Brylcreemed hair and wearing brothel-creepers moved in time to the swaying and gyrating of the ride as they collected fares with the efficiency of vergers at a church service. There was, of course Gypsy Rosa Lee, with her last year, this year and next year's predictions – "Beware of a neighbour with an 'E' in his name."

It was an event not to be missed, but Alan knew that he must find a last minute excuse to avoid going, because the more frequent the arranged meeting between himself and Anne of Cleves, the more difficult it would be when both sets of parents realised that nothing would come of it, His own parents must be, if not altogether disappointed by the appearance of Mavis Pickersgill, certainly surprised. So plain. Not even ugly – just downright plain.

That night, as he lay in bed, Alan had a mental image of what she'd look like several years hence. Straggle hair, wearing a wrap-round pinnie, and probably two snotty-nosed kids under her feet. Then he imagined Rosemary Beaumont (as he hoped she would be). Still beautiful, with off-spring at grammar school prior to university, and secure in both finance and love.

There was no comparison. No competition. It was Rosemary Beaumont or nobody.

Chapter 12

It was Monday morning, the annual Wakes Weeks holiday a thing of the past. In the Boothroyd van were clean overalls, ham and beetroot sandwiches, on top of which sat a slice of cake (which dad always referred to as 'a jockey') It was work as usual.

" Good Morning, Mr Boothroyd," Alan called to his employer, then, seeing the love of his life, he politely greeted her with, "Good morning, Rosemary."

"Good morning, Alan."

He sighed. "Back to the old routine."

"Did you have a nice holiday?" she put on a brave act.

"Oh, a super time. Absolute paradise."

"Really? And where was that?"

He parried her innocent chatter. "Beside the seaside."

"And would you be – " but their banter was interrupted by the arrival of the firm's junior partner. Alan, temporarily stunned stared at the black eye and split lip, as Basil Boothroyd came into the office. "This is nothing compared to what the other bloke got. I'll bet he's still in hospital," he boasted, "I really did make mincemeat out of him. He'll think twice before he smacks me in the mouth again."

"But when did – ?"

"It's a long story, Alan, you don't need to know all the details this morning, we'll natter later, but before then, dad wants a word with us all. The other fellers are waiting, let's join them."

They went into the yard where the owner of Boothroyds was looking through the documents in his hands, despite having read the several times. The two apprentices, Jim Watson who had been with the firm for over thirty years were waiting, and now the complete work force was present the owner cleared his throat then addressed his audience. "Nah then, a bit o' good news. Boothroyds 'ave landed a big job, an' ah've put an advert in 'Chronicle in 'situations vacant column fer sum more staff. We'll be workin' in two teams. Jim's in charge o' one, Basil the other, but we'll all on us need ter instruct any new fellers we get into 'Boothroyd ways o' doin' things. But if this all goes well, it could just the start o' bigger things ter come. There'll be overtime ee and bonuses paid. Nah, yer all know where yer goin' this mornin' an' yer work's planned out fer 'week. Let's get to it."

Alan looked again at the black eye, puzzled, but his workmate said no more than "Call round this evening, we'll go for a drink."

Her son's bruised face was causing speculation and intrigue for the driving force behind Boothroyd and Son, and she paused from her Monday morning chores and pondered on what escapade had resulted in this temporary disfigurement.

Probably some husband seeking revenge, or it could be even – but nothing, absolutely nothing would surprise her any more.

Her offspring were entire opposites.

She'd a son who led a truly immoral life, and a daughter who – well, Rosemary had not yet confided in her mother regarding her holiday romance, but Constance was certain that an announcement would soon be in the paper, and pictures in the Yorkshire Post and Yorkshire Life confirming the engagement of their daughter to… but she didn't know who the lucky man was. Perhaps the son of an MP, but an Earl or a Lord would be better. The Boothroyd's would have arrived!

She stopped daydreaming. All would be revealed in good time, but until then there were more pressing matters.

Extra staff would mean more wages to do, perhaps necessitating her being in the office for two mornings a week, and next month rehearsals would begin for the Operatic Society's forthcoming production. It was to be Gilbert and Sullivan's 'The Gondoliers' and auditions were to be held the following Monday evening after the first rehearsal. This was to hoodwink any new members into thinking that 'all were equal' –but the principals had already been chosen. The Gondoliers was cast.

John Roberts, small and agile would play The Duke of Plaza Toro, while Susan Schofield at well over eighteen stone would play the Duchess. There was only one contender for the role of Marco, for a powerful tenor voice was needed to 'Take a pair of Sparkling eyes', the other principal roles being chosen from established members . The part of Luiz would be played by the son of one of the society's ex-presidents. The lad could neither sing nor act, but being the Duke's private drummer, he'd be able to 'bang on a drum' if nothing else. The show was more or less cast, before the so-called 'auditions' would take place.

Constance had persuaded the Society's committee members that this was the ideal choice of operetta. But had not mentioned her reason for choosing Gilbert and Sullivan, for it was a show that needed absolutely no interference from the Glamorous Night(and she must have given 'glamorous nights' to hundreds of fellers) or Perchance to Scream and various other names she now gave Miss Bluebell. Nor could the baggage claim that she'd been on friendly terms with the liberettist or composer, unless one saw her without the garish make-up and realised what an old dear she really was.

Not even a 'has- been' – more a 'never-was'.

Oh no, when she accepted that she was being ignored she would lose interest, or move to some other town where she could try to assert her influence. For Constance Boothroyd ruled the town's Operatic Society, and would not be upstaged by Miss Bluebell or anyone else.

Round the corner from the Boothroyd residence the two young men swapped their seats, Alan became the passenger, Basil the driver.

"Where are we heading?"

"Oh, somewhere very quiet, not in town, even."

"We could go to the pub at Castle Hill, nobody will be lurking there – but how did it happen?" and Alan pointed to the bruises. "It's mad, getting into a fight, unless I'm with you. We're mates, I don't want someone knocking hell out of you when you're on your own," and

Alan felt suddenly protective toward his best mate, and (he hoped) his future brother-in-law.

"Well," and Basil erred on the side of caution, "let's get to the pub, and over a drink we'll… put the world to rights, so to speak."

"Mmm. And if I find out the bloke who did this to you I'll – "

"Alan, it's sorted."

The younger of the two men knew when to speak his mind, and also knew the value of silence… He tried to change the subject, but couldn't think of anything to say. Their destination was miles away, and quite remote. To have agreed to Alan's suggestion Basil must be in real trouble.

"Well, come on then. What you been up to?"

"Well, not 'me' exactly – us!"

"Eh?"

"Our 'fun' on the way to Holmfirth."

"But we were careful, we took precautions."

"Oh, they're not in the club or anything, it's just that one of them told her brother about us… and…"

"Yes?"

"He was seeking revenge for our 'ruining' his innocent little sister – and he's looking for you as well, so be on your guard."

"Thanks for warning me."

"But he'll think twice before he tries anything on after the belting I gave him – and I kicked him where it hurts most. The contents of his scrotum will probably be pulp from now on."

"Bloody hell! Is that why he's in hospital?"

"Among other things. A few broken ribs, you know, and – but he started it. Doesn't like a feller having fun with his sister."

Alan finished his drink, and wondered if Basil himself would feel as protective toward his own sister, and beat the living daylights out of any man who'd been monkeying around. It was not a pleasant thought.

"Anyway," and a plan was suddenly forming in his mind, "at the weekend, what say we have a lads night away from it all? Even go to

Blackpool, for instance, to look at the local talent at the *Winter Gardens* ballroom. How does that grab you?"

Basil considered, as Alan went on to explain. "My parents have 'something planned' for me, and I need to have a get-out."

"Ok, a lad's weekend away from everything."

"Yes," Alan agreed. They needed a fool-proof plan. He'd need to tell Basil exactly what to say to his parents. It had to seem genuine and convincing.

He jumped up to answer the knock on the door, and in pretended surprise greeted the caller with "Why hallo Basil, and what brings you to this neck of the woods?"

"If I could just come inside," but he was already in the kitchen. He nodded to the man in the armchair. " 'Evening, Mr Beaumont. I'm sorry to burst in on you like this, but..." and he shrugged his shoulders, "with you not being on the phone I couldn't..."

"Oh, that's all reight, lad."

Alan's mother, who had by now joined them smiled at their caller and asked,"D'yer want a cup o' tea? I'm just brewin' up. It's Basil, isn't it?"

"Yes, that'd be grand, Mrs. Beaumont. Thanks very much."

"Now,"and Alan did his best to look truly bewildered, "to what do we owe this visit?"

"Well," and the guest made himself comfortable in the vacant armchair beside the fire, "it's to do with this new job Boothroyds have landed."

"Summatt gooan wrong?"

"No, quite the opposite. I don't know, Mr Beaumont, if Alan's mentioned it to you, but we've secured a big contract. Dad's put an advert in the local paper for some extra staff, and... well, we seem to be working all hours in preparation. That's why..." and he paused for effect, "I have to see various individuals this weekend."

"Extra overtime," Alan joked.

"It could be – for you. You see," he explained to suddenly interested parents, "I can't drive at the moment, which is why I've had to come here on the bus tonight, but it's going to be a long and hectic weekend, which is why I wondered if you'd be free, Alan, so's you could drive me around? We'll go in my car, of course, but I'll have to be the passenger, and it might even mean a stay overnight – but Boothroyds will pay any hotel expenses , because there's no telling when those I need to call on will be at home, or available to discuss things, or even – "

"Yes, of course I'll help," Alan broke in, "after all, I may not be able to drive you round in… a couple of months, say. And I have a sort of 'loyalty' to your dad. I'm more than happy to help for as long as I can, and in any way I can."

"Thanks. You're a pal. And we won't mention it, not even to dad at this stage, because he's got more than enough to cope with at the moment."

"Is yer mum all reight?" Gladys Beaumont asked, even though she scarcely knew the woman.

"Mmm. Singing. Every evening! And Rosemary has been commandeered as accompanist. If the wind's in the right direction you'll probably hear them even though we live miles away."

"As bad as that?" Alan commiserated with him.

"Oh Alan, it's bloody awful. She's singing at some Harvest Festival, it's a yearly thing mother does. Then there's the occasional *Messiah* at Huddersfield Town Hall, and carol concerts at Christmas. I shall be glad when it's January."

"I 'ope Alan's aunt Ada Martha isn't the organist. She 'its so many wrong notes shu could be playin' owt. If shu is, it could be a reight performance," and Alan's mother shook her head.

"Mmm," then Basil suddenly asked, "I'm not… er, I mean, you haven't anything planned this evening have you, Alan? You don't have a date, or anything?"

"No, nothing in that department, now or in the immediate future."

"Well, d'you fancy… a pint at your local? What about you, Mr Beaumont, would you like to join us? And perhaps your mum, as well?"

"Aye, that'd be champion, but ah mun get changed first," and she touched her permed hair as she spoke.

Alan collected the empty mugs. Basil kept giving his workmate an inquisitive stare, but seeing the satisfied look on his face, knew the evening had been a success.

"But yer'll nooan be able ter go ter Shatt Fair – an' what abaht Mavis?" and now Alan had returned from taking his workmate home what he was anticipating was being played out

"Well, when Basil turned up on the doorstep to ask for my help, what could I do?"

"But 'Pickergill's are expectin' us."

"Well, you and mum go – and you never know, Basil might see all the people he needs to in good time, and I could still get to Skelmanthorpe… late evening."

"Well," and his father gave a defeated look, "if that's 'best yer can cum up wi'."

"What else do you want? When Basil asked me to chauffer him around you ought to have said that it wasn't on."

"Nay, ah dooant want ter interfere in yer work routine – but it's 'weekend, an that's yours ter do as yer please."

"And I am doing. Don't you see, dad, both Mr and Mrs. Boothroyd have been very kind, and Mr Boothroyd's been a very considerate and generous employer. It's my way of repaying them."

"There's nowt else ter say, then."

"There'll be other weekends," Alan tried to lessen the disappointment on his father's face, "and as I said, I might get there before… well, I can always walk round the fair proper and look for you."

"Aye, we mun leave it at that. Turn 'light aht affore yer cum ter bed, an mak' sure all's switched off." And realising that further words would be meaningless, his father took off his shoes before ascending the dark-brown-where-it-was-threadbare stairs carpet.

Rosemary Boothroyd, though not 'worried' was nevertheless deep in thought, as, her make-up removed, she stared into her mirror. The unforgiving light showed a face where lines no longer hidden would become more pronounced as the years progressed. Expensive creams and the like if seeming successful were only temporary, at best merely retarding what would inevitably occur.

She'd wake up one morning, her youth gone.

She'd be a middle aged, probably single woman! But that was in the future, she told herself, though she would be thirty at the end of the month. Lots of women her age were married with a couple of children. Others were married, divorced and ready to take on husband number two – and she'd not found number one, yet.

Oh, there'd been several young (and not so young) men in her life, but none of them had offered marriage. Romantic liasons, yes, but the thing, the commitment she needed most, it hadn't happened. Or had it, and she wouldn't accept it?

Her thoughts went to an old flame Ian Barlow who mother took an instant dislike to because he had ginger hair. What difference did that make to a person? But her mother was quite adamant, he was not 'the one'. Then there was John Ingham who worked at the bank, and who, according to her mother was painstakingly (and without the Boothroyd permission) looking through their savings and investment accounts in order to decide if such a family were suitable for a marriage proposal. There had been others, but none of them had, in her mother's eyes been suitable, and, Rosemary supposed, if Alan should pursue his amorous advances, then what hope or future could such a romance have? An employee who would (according to mother) undoubtedly have his eye on the main chance, marriage merely being a way to becoming a junior partner in the family firm, equal to Basil, the son and heir.

No, if her mother's eyes that would not be acceptable.

And Rosemary tried yet again to convince herself, if Alan was about to go in the army for a couple of years, why, anything could happen during that time. He'd not want to come home and marry a woman in her thirties as she'd be then. No, he'd want someone young and attractive. Anything so permanent as marriage between the two of them was out of the question.

As he slowly undressed, Alan Beaumont congratulated both himself and his workmate on the convincing lies they had told in order to get away for the weekend.

Away from the Pickergills (who would probably have the keys to the property two doors from their home) which they were hoping to tempt as a sort of dowry for anyone daft and desperate enough to wed their daughter.

He supposed his dad would, the following day, explain to his workmate that 'things' had cropped up workwise for Alan, and it would be early evening before he could join them. Both sets of parents living in hopes was, he decided, kinder than a blunt refusal and – well, when he was at sea and out of the way, then the whole thing would somehow be 'washed away'. Mavis would marry some lad who worked in the pit, her parents would be happy, and that would be the end of that.

But his own future seemed, at best, unpredictable, for what his call-up papers came, what happened then?

He supposed that on the appointed day he'd present himself at some army camp or military base, and there'd be forms, lots of questions, a medical, and perhaps at that point he'd be able to state his preference as to which of the armed services he'd like to join. He pondered again about the air-force, but felt drawn to the Navy – yes, the navy, definitely.

Not that it would be at all like it was romanticised. No, there'd be cleaners, cooks, bottle-washers, pen-pushers – he didn't for a single moment imagine that he'd be called upon to help paint (in order to disguise) some military vessel before it sailed into enemy waters, its object being to collect valuable information on which Britain's stability and supremacy would depend.

No, that sort of stuff was reserved for films and best-sellers.

He climbed into bed, it was time to get some rest.

Chapter 13

"Bracing Blackpool."

"Bloody freezing Blackpool, more like," the junior partner of Boothroyds replied to his friend's statement.

"Aye 'summer's over."

"Still," Basil pointed out, "we haven't come to sunbathe."

"No. More to escape."

"This bird," and Basil paused to light his cigarette, "she's not up the duff, is she, because if she is, Annie could – "

"What, with a face like she has? No," Alan assured him. "At least, if she is it's not mine. It'd take a braver man than me to mount that. She really is an unattractive cow."

"And yet… your parent s think a marriage could result?"

"When hell freezes over. I think… oh lord, I don't know how to tell them, but – "

"You need to kill it right at the start."

"Well, that's what I am doing."

"And now," and his mate took command, "a walk on the Golden Mile, then a drink and a bite to eat, and back to the hotel, a shit, shave and shower, change into some decent gear, a couple of drinks in Yates Wine Lodge, then Winter Gardens Ballroom, here we come."

It was, fortunately for the younger of the two, an uneventful evening, for it seemed that the girls were there simply to dance and not hoping for romantic liaisons, or even half an hour's slap-and-tickle – not that Alan was into such things any more.

No, it was Rosemary Boothroyd – or a life of celibacy. He shuddered when he thought of the disgusting way he and Basil had carried on with the girls little more than strangers. But that was all in his shameful past. Even if he were even vaguely religious he'd ask God to forgive him.

But he wasn't, so he couldn't!

It was the last waltz. A girl he'd been dancing with earlier looked at him hopefully. He purposely turned away. It was the time for future dates, when promises were made, and hands were allowed to stray. But not tonight.

Basil, on the ballroom floor was holding his partner close. Alan saw her shake her head, there was nothing being promised in that department either, and as the music died away the dancers cleared the floor, and the two men made their retreat.

Back at their hotel, after a quick drink they retired, Alan feeling somehow strange sharing sleeping quarters (even though they were in a twin-bedded room) with another man. There was no 'embarrassment' in seeing each other naked, and Alan told himself that on board ship he'd be sleeping alongside loads of fellers, some complete strangers, not like his room-mate for the night, his best mate and, hopefully, future brother-in-law.

"It's been a hectic weekend," Alan lied to his parents, "but I think Basil's seen all interested parties."

" 'Interested parties'? – an' what abaht last neet's party as didn't go off as earlier expected? What 'Pickergills'll think abaht us, ah dooant know."

"Well." Alan reasoned, "you explained, didn't you, that it was just one of those things."

"Oh aye," and his father paused to draw breath, then continued, "we need ter 'ave a reight talk, young man."

"Leeave it terneet," his wife pleaded, "ah dooant want ony bother between yer."

"There'll be no 'bother' as yer put it, but there's things as mun be said. We need ter know where we stand, all on us."

"So… what's on your mind, dad?"

"Yer know damned well. Me an' yer mam, we've booath 'ad ter work 'ard all us lives. We want summatt better for us only lad – an' if yer can marry inter money? – well, it doesn't want dismissin' lightly."

"If you mean who I think you mean… well, we hardly know one another. All right, I accept that you work with her father and the two of you are best mates – and on the coalface I'm sure you do need someone to depend on, if things should go wrong. But at the same time, you can't expect me to sacrifice my life for the promise of a down payment on a terrace house, and in the very distant future some nest egg from the sale of a pub. I want something more than that." He thought again about Rosemary Boothroyd, then blurted out, "I want love."

"Well g'ie it time, an' you an' Mavis, who knows?"

"No, not with Mavis."

"Shu's a grand lass – an' nooan sort as'll go wi' other men."

"I agree with you there. With a face like she has, she wouldn't get the bloody chance. She's not just plain – she's downright ugly."

"See, yer young bugger, yer'd better get ter bed affore we say things as we'll later regret."

"Yer dad's tryin' ter do 'is best for yer," his mother tried to calm down what was quickly becoming a volatile situation, " 'ee's thinkin abaht yer own good."

"Then he must stop trying to barter me off in the marriage stakes. He's too late, anyway."

"Eh?"

"I've had enough tonight. I'm going to bed."

He lay awake, listening to the noise from the kitchen, then after what seemed an eternity, the sound of footsteps on the stairs as his parents came to bed. The was the usual opening and closing of the bedroom door, then the sound from the bathroom of the toilet flushing, then there was a tapping on his door. He ignored it, and when his mother approached his bed he pretended to be asleep.

It was easier that way, because there was nothing more to say. But what could he possibly say that could righten what was becoming an impossible situation?

His parents should have by now realised that any relationship between himself and the daughter of his father's workmate was dead before it had even begun. Again he thought of Henry the Eighth and the Flanders Mare. He could understand the necessity for the union between the king and whoever his ministers chose as a diplomatic measure, but his own situation was entirely different.

He did not have to marry for England – he'd marry for love!

He dressed quickly then crept downstairs to grab a bite to eat and make a sandwich for lunch. He glanced at the clock, he could be away before his parents stirred. Dad was on the afternoon shift, which meant he left home to catch the twenty minutes to one bus to the pit, arriving home around half nine in the evening.

His work routine alternated between what was referred to as 'mornin's' when he was up at the crack of dawn, then two weeks later 'afternooin shift, as was today, and his routine followed a strict pattern.

In the privacy of the hallway he'd change into his pit-clothes, and before leaving would shove his 'snap' down his shirt front. This could consist of sausages cooked the day before, split lengthwise and placed between thick slices of bread then smothered in HP sauce, or beef dripping sandwiches with sliced pickled onions. They'd be wrapped up in well-used greaseproof paper, the 'jokey' on top, then the whole lot tied up in a red handkerchief with white spots in.

There'd also be a flask of strong tea with no milk but lots of sugar which he'd shove in his overcoat pocket, and before actually leaving to catch the bus he'd put on his knee-caps, clogs and hard miner's helmet, then on arriving at the pit itself, after collecting his lamp and descending into the bowels of the earth it would be a ride on 'the Paddy' to the coal-face proper, where he'd be the deputy or shot-firer, depending on which shift days of afternoons he was on.

Father and son would hardly see one another till the weekend, and Alan hoped that by then things might have calmed down. He didn't like arguing with his parents, neither did he like being dictated to, but there must be a way – even if it meant agreeing to their plans until… well, he'd be out from under their feet very soon.

He shoved his overalls and other things he might need into the Boothroyd and Son decorators van, and closed the kitchen door quietly, after first dropping the latch. Another working week was about to begin.

The Boothroyd clan were there when he arrived. The owner deliberating on who should do what, Basil smoking and Rosemary in the yard with a bundle of papers in her hand, while her mother, from the office window surveyed the scene and mentally noted whatever she might need to draw to her husband's attention when the time presented itself. A lot of standing about doing nothing, she decided, looking at the Boothroyd staff.

Two young apprentices fooling about like silly schoolboys, the junior partner just staring into space – oh, there'd be an alteration when the new staff were engaged. There'd be no standing about idling, it would be down to work the second they arrived.

Then she noticed Alan. He seemed to be giving her daughter curious glances, almost as though – but she was imagining things. She must be.

In the Beaumont household it was a week of being extremely polite to one another, and careful not to offend or say a word out of place.

When Alan could he drove to the pit to collect his dad from the afternoon shift, and thought yet again, what a bloody awful life it must be, working on the coalface. He'd drive past the manager's office on his left, now in darkness, while as he neared the pit proper, still black from their shift and looking like tame gorillas the miners clattered over the cobbles. From the main shaft there was a diffused yellow light where even more gorillas escaped from the pit cage itself. There was yet another light from what dad had years earlier described as 'lamp oyle' which was where the miners lamps were housed when not being actually used. There was also a sort of 'savoury fog' coming from the canteen where a bright light shone as Nellie Summerscales wiped down the tables and searched for bits of discarded food or cutlery that had escaped earlier washing up. The canteen was closed, but the smell lingered.

There was also a bicycle shed, a car park being unnecessary, for miners and cars were not a marriage. Alan would look around him, a sinking feeling hitting his stomach. Oh, it must be a bloody awful life, he wouldn't wish it on his worst enemy, yet his own father was wanting, planning, this for him. He thought of earlier revelations by aunt Muriel that his father had been making tentative enquiries on his behalf, and that, in his words, "it's all bin settled."

Fortunately dad had not broached this subject, and Alan hoped he wouldn't.

Chapter 14

It was Saturday.

A day when mum would take stock of what was in the pantry and the fridge before announcing, "ah'm goin' on 'two o'clock bus ter get 'week's shoppin' – is there owt yer fancy, 'pair o' yer?"

"Sum sausages," came the reply, but dad always asked for sausages.

"An' Alan? Owt?"

"No, whatever you get'll be OK. But I'm going to the match, so it'll save you going on the bus if you come in the van."

"That'll be grand. Eee, it 'as it's benefits, bein' driver fer Booithroyds."

He nodded. It was late morning, mum was preparing lunch when Walt Wagstaff the postman came up the path. "A fair do, terday," he boasted, shoving a handful of envelopes into the waiting hands.

"Ah'm certain he nobbutt delivers stuff once a week, what's 'ee got fer us this mornin'?" And Gladys Beaumont paused from slicing carrots.

"Oh, it all looks summatt an' nowt. There's 'lectric bill, they read 'meter last week, an' there's – oh, this is fer you, lad," and his father handed him an official looking buff envelope with the word *private* on the back – the thing his parents had been dreading, and it was now in his hands!

Alan Beaumont read, then re-read, then stared at it for a long time before announcing, "It's arrived."

"Bloody 'ell."

"We mun do summatt," Gladys Beaumont waved her hand across her face as her breathing became laboured. "We can't 'ave our lad blown ter bits in sum foreign country."

"Mum, that won't happen."

"Cum on, sit thissen dahn an' pull thissen tergether. We've been expectin' this fer sum time, nah."

"Ah know – but ah nivver though as it'd 'appen. An' on a weekend, an'all. When ah get 'old o' Walt Wagstgaff, ah'll – "

"Mum, calm down."

"It's all reight sayin'calm dahn, but there's nobbutt one way aht, an that's goin' dahn 'pit wi' yer dad. What did 'pit manager say when yer asked abaht Alan working wi yer?"

Her husband gave a sigh. "Said there'd be no guarantee as we'd be on 'same coil face, or 'same shift even… but…" then he turned to his son. "Yer can see what a state yer mam's in. Are yer goin' ter be sensible an' – "

"And what if I do as you both want… and there's an explosion down the pit? There's a feller lives in Lepton who got his hand blown off when there was a pit accident. These things do happen. Working on the coalface has certain dangers attached to it."

"Nooan 'same as bein' in as war zone where men are shooitin' one another. Believe me lad, yer safer in 'pit."

Alan looked at his mother. She'd gone a sort of puffy red, obviously having breathing difficulties, and was near to tears. "Please, Alan," she pleaded, "at least, say yer'll think abaht it."

"An' yer'd better' mak' yer mind up affore – "

"It's the twenty third of next month," and Alan looked again at the printed form. "It states a time and a place, and – well, I'll read it through carefully tonight when I come home from the match."

"Yer still goin' ter watch fooitball?" his father stared, unable to believe what his son was contemplating.

"Well, why not? This letter isn't the end of the world. Hundreds, thousands of lads will have received the same. Some this morning, even."

It would seem, and he perused the morning's communication later that evening in his bedroom, eighteen months in a branch of the Armed Forces and on a reserve list for the following four years when his unit could be re-called for up to twenty days but on no more than three occasions during the four year period.

There would be a medical examination, and the recruit would also sit an exam which was like an intelligence test, and at that point asked which service, Army, Navy or Air Force, they wanted to go into, the choice been dependent and influenced by the results of the intelligence test.

He wished he could somehow contact his uncle Ben to ask him about his days in the RAF, but of course, that was during the Second World War. It would be different in peacetime, but his uncle had completely disappeared from the family scene, so he was unable to pursue that road. Alan marvelled at his having the guts to rebel against what was a several generation family tradition, for it must have been ten times more difficult for him that what was facing his nephew, yet time was no longer on his side, for the actual summons would arrive a few weeks after the medical, and be delivered by the postman in a plain brown envelope, with instructions when and where the prospective recruit had to report to barracks for the start of the ten weeks basic training, the first day of the soldiering always being on a Thursday.

It seemed most of the lads went into the army, the Royal Navy taking only around five per-cent of the numbers available. He hoped he'd be lucky when the time came, nor would he be necessarily 'at sea' for there were several on-shore bases, and so many various jobs to do.

"And the medical's a bloody scream," Basil warned him, on knowing that he'd soon be experiencing this. "Done strictly to King's Regulations, and ends up with a young lady doctor asking you to cough after you've dropped your trousers."

"Eh?"

"You wait and see," he laughed. "It's 'drop 'em, cough. You're in'."

"Thanks for warning me."

"And you don't need it to 'rise to the occasion'."

"Depends on what the young lady doctor's like," Alan parried his banter.

They stopped further joking; there was the week's work to organise.

She gave a wistful smile… and remembered.

Afternoons of making love, nights of unbridled passion as Alan –

"Can we do that again, Rosemary? We'll take it from," and her mother's voice brought her away from lovemaking and to the task in hand. She pointed to the music. "Yes, beginning 'their loud uplifted angels' trumpets'."

"And you're going slightly sharp on 'angels'. I'll just play it for you."

Being her rehearsal accompanist was one of the rare moments when the daughter could correct her mother , but, Constance consoled herself, the accompanist did not actually produce the notes, or the pitch – they were part of the Steinway and needed only to be hit.

"I'll play it again," Rosemary offered. 'Uplifted angels' trumpets blow'. Her fingers tapped out the notes, then mother and daughter resumed their rendition of Handel's *Let the Bright Seraphim.*

Again Constance told herself that Rosemary should have pursued a pianistic career instead of being a typist and secretary. Such musical talent did mother and daughter have – and for nothing more than Harvest Festivals and the like.

Such a waste – such a terrible waste!

Yet it gave them a mother and daughter 'bonding', their love of music, and Constance hoped that, as it was drawing them close, then her daughter would confide in her about her latest romance. For Constance knew – oh, she knew – that a man was lurking somewhere in the background.

Now, who that man was, (or what he was) still remained a mystery. Obviously a man in his… early thirties and already a success in his chosen career… which was? – well, that was one of the things that needed to be taken into consideration before he could be officially welcomed into the Boothroyd household.

Also his financial status – and his own family. What sort of a background did he have? A public school education? A distinguished army career? – or was he, as she earlier imagined (and hoped) a member of the aristocracy? The eldest son who would one day inherit the family title (but not, she hoped, the family debts). She again made a mental note of those she must invite to the wedding, some members of the Masonic Lodge, their friends in the local Conservative Association – and as an after-thought she might also include their MP. It would give the occasion even more class, when it actually happened.

Yet her daughter was keeping things very secret, which caused her mother to wonder why. If anything was to materialise, then it had to become, if not 'common' knowledge, certainly family knowledge. Children could be such a –

"And you're still slightly sharp," and Rosemary again played the phrase, "It's on 'Angels' trumpets'."

"Sorry dear, I'm miles away. Let's do it again, from the beginning."

Chapter 15

He arrived home early, he'd need a quick bath and a shave, then after a bite to eat he'd get into his smart outfit. Burton copper bronze suit, pale blue shirt, and because it was an 'occasion' he'd wear the bow tie that had not been out of its box, even.

"Will yer be late 'ome?" his mum asked.

"Er..." he considered, "I could be, but I've got the latch key with the keys for the van, so that's OK."

"An' be careful. Dooant get ter much ter drink."

"Don't worry. It'll be shandys, and not many of them."

"Eee, it seems funny, socialisin' in 'middle o' week."

"Well, it's just a 'one off'."

"An'... I might call an' see yer aunt Muriel. Yer dad'll nooan be 'ome till late, bein' on 'afternooin shift."

"I'll drop you off if you want, but I must get changed now or I'll be late and might miss all the best bits."

Even he didn't know what the 'best bits' were – but he didn't want to miss them.

The party had already begun!

The Boothroyd staff tending to congregate among themselves, the Boothroyd friends standing and chattering in select groups, while positioned near the door so that she could personally meet and greet the guests was Constance Boothroyd herself. It was quite an occasion, the twins thirtieth birthday!

Her husband was with his staff, daughter in conversation with her aunt Violet, her father's youngest sister, and coming through the door to the private function room of the George Hotel (and looking very smart) was Alan Beaumont.

"Alan, how very nice to see you," the hostess greeted him.

He looked around, two presents in his hands. "Where's… er… the man of the moment?" and he held forward what was obviously a bottle of something.

"Basil will be along shortly, he's had to call and 'see someone', as he put it."

"And Rosemary?"

She pointed in her daughter's direction.

"Then I'll just go and give her these and wish her a happy birthday," and he waved what the hostess imagined to be a box of chocolates.

"You're looking quite immaculate this evening," she complimented him.

"Thank you," and he moved toward the young woman in the slinky evening gown. "Rosemary," he made a big show of kissing her on her cheek, "Happy Twenty-first."

"Again?"

"Well, you only look… you know… twenty one."

"You say the nicest things," then she whispered, "Mr Hunter."

"And these are for you," and he gave her the present wrapped in fancy paper and tied with a red ribbon. "And this is also for you," and suddenly serious he removed the item from his jacket pocket and slipped the box into her hand. "Don't open it in full view of everybody, but you've probably guessed what's inside. Think about it carefully, and if I see one morning that it's on your finger then I'll know that you've accepted my offer of marriage."

"Oh Alan… and tonight, of all nights."

"Please… just put it safe for now, and say you'll consider it. I'm not a millionaire, but I'm offering something more precious than money. I'm offering undying love!"

"Give me… time."

"Mmm."

"And now," and she preened herself, "you can buy me a birthday drink."

The waiter was hovering, Alan attracted his attention and the two of them continued in polite conversation as Constance Boothroyd looked on. Some more family friends arrived, the hostess glanced at her watch. In less the thirty minutes the evening meal – and then her son arrived, and Constance Boothroyed froze – for with him was the baggage!

Constance wanted to march across and tell her this was a private function, admittance by invitation only, but she knew that would be of no use.

How her son was in any way associated with such a person was quite beyond her – and the two of them were now standing in front of her, the Glamorous Night smiling. There must be no scene, not in front of the Boothroyd friends and staff, that would undoubtedly come later.

"Constance – how very nice to meet you socially."

"Really?" and Constance Boothroyd turned the other way.

War had now been declared!

The baggage deserved all that Constance could throw at her.

It was not by mere chance that she had become acquainted, and on what Constance imagined 'intimate' terms with her son, but it was the start of something carefully organised and to a specific end, but as to what, Constance was unsure. Throughout the meal Constance took sidelong glances at the gold lame revealing too much cleavage, the garish make-up, and hair lacquered till it was like steel with not a strand out of place. Old mutton parading as lamb.

Yes, that summed her up to a tee!

Her son, like a lovesick swain was dancing attendance on her, and Constance felt like giving him a damned good smack across the face before calling for one of the waiters to forcefully remove that which was annoying her. But what would happen if she did?

The Careless Rupture really had crossed the line, she deserved whatever punishment Constance was able to inflict.

There were more pressing matters to be dealt with. Basil would need to see a doctor privately, and without delay.

There was, she had earlier been given to believe, something politely referred to as a 'Special Clinic' at the local hospital the third Thursday of each month, but if he were seen by the other patients (and of course, he would be), how could he claim that his being there was quite innocent?

No, he couldn't!

And besides, being in a waiting room and in such close proximity to the town's prostitutes and outrageous homosexuals wearing make-up, and probably womens undergarments, he could possibly catch something from the very breath they exhaled. There were also, she had on good authority, even vicars who claimed to have caught something from dirty lavatory seats while using public toilets, and very worried young men who had 'a rash' and feared they'd not be able to father children, for they foolishly imagined it to be the onset of some venereal disease.

But if they chose to consort with harlots and perverts, then they deserved all they got – And her own son could be part of this scum – oh, what a depraved, disgusting young man he was!

The twins thirtieth birthday. Some party it had turned out to be. She thought of the party at *The George* several years previously, when Basil had returned from his eighteen months' National Service, a 'welcome home' party, and also to celebrate his being made a junior partner in the firm. But this evening's fiasco? – well, it would be the last one she'd ever organise.

And her other disappointment had to be her daughter, Rosemary. Her mother had (foolishly) imagined that her daughter would have as her escort the young man she was in love with – but it hadn't happened. He lover, the aristocrat, was still a secret.

It was at times like these she felt she needed to 'get away from it all' with perhaps a nice holiday in Cliftonville, or even a cruise, but such things were not possible with the new staff and workload.

Besides, if she were away for any length of time there was no telling what her offspring could get up to. They were more difficult to control now than when they were children.

No – they were impossible, absolutely impossible to control.

In the privacy of her bedroom. Rosemary opened the box that Alan had given her earlier, it contained, as she expected, an engagement ring.

A single diamond, but it must have cost him a fortune – yet when he found out, would he still want to marry her? Besides, he could soon be in… Germany, or if he were serious about becoming a sailor then he could be in the middle of the Atlantic Ocean, or on a battleship heading goodness knows where. A long engagement? – it could be years, throughout which time her mother would do nothing but natter. It was something she was very good at. That, and getting her own way.

Slowly she took the ring from its box and slipped it on the third finger of her left hand. It suited her. A single diamond!

A love token.

She'd keep it hidden until – well, she and Alan needed to have a serious talk, and the sooner the better – and there was something else . It had been puzzling her all evening – her brother and his guest.

Older than he was, very flamboyant, and there was 'something' about her that her mother had found distasteful, and made obvious. It were almost as though – but she had enough to occupy her mind without worrying about Brother Fartiarse.

Chapter 16

Every detail was as he'd expected, even down to the medical that Basil had earlier and jokingly described. Some of the fellers seemed surprised, one or two even shocked, and he thought one lad was going to burst into tears.

But that was all behind him, he was on his way home, and sitting upstairs on the bus he had time to think. Was he embarking on something he'd have no control over? If so, would he be better working alongside his father? Should he settle for the simple life, and even think again about courting, and eventually marrying, the Flanders Mare?

He must stop referring to her as that, it wasn't at all complimentary – but what about Rosemary?

Each morning he looked hopefully at her left hand. The third finger was missing something. A statement that she was promised in marriage.

Unless he had a rival?

Was there another feller hovering in the background?

Someone who might have money, a fast car… and be more restrained in his lovemaking than he and Rosemary had been. A once a fortnight man instead of six times a night with other things for encores. Oh, the marvellous fortnight they'd spent together as Mr and Mrs Hunter. But that was all over, and even at the birthday celebration at the *George,* she'd been cool toward him. Yet perhaps she wasn't expecting a proposal of marriage. But it would have been a party to remember if she'd flashed it on her finger and announced to all concerned that she and Alan were an item.

He imagined his future mother-in-law would have had words to say – she might still have, if ever she were to find out about the holiday fortnight – and as for his own parents? Well, they'd met her twin on several occasions and seemed to get on. But introducing Rosemary to the family as his future wife? That could present problems, as they'd been expecting romance to blossom between himself and Mavis (and he mustn't call her *that* any more), would they take kindly to some other girl who had won his affections?

The boss's daughter! – He could just imagine the sly innuendos from both sets of parents.

Basil would be OK with the arrangement, but he imagined Lady Boothroyd would look on their marriage as a way of him getting a firm foot in a very lucrative family business. A mere tradesman marrying their daughter? Oh no, such a union was far beneath what her mother had planned.

He lit a cigarette. They were on the outskirts of the town and would soon be pulling into the bus station. From there he'd walk down to Lord Street where, and he glanced at his watch, the Barnsley bus would be waiting. It had been a traumatic day, he'd be glad to get home.

"Nah then lad, 'ow've yer gooan on?"

"Oh, you know – but it'll be several weeks before I hear anything definite."

"Aye," his father replied, "but 'ave yer decided on 'army or 'navy?"

"If all goes well, the navy – but of course, with so many naval bases around the coast I could be… a sailor who never goes to sea."

"Safer that way."

"Not so much fun, though. Anyway, we must wait and see."

"Yer mam's gooan ter 'club whist-drive."

"Oh."

"It seems a popular thing, nah. Twenty-four 'ands, an' ten an' six fer 'winner. What yer goin' ter do terneet, then? Watch tele, or … ?"

"I might go into town and see if I can find Basil. He'll want to know if everything went as he described it," and he thought again about the medical. "Drop 'em, cough," were Basil's words, and he was correct.

A quick wash and change and he'd be away, but he hesitated as to where in town he would be going exactly. He'd look first in the Royal George, then the Horse and Griffin, but he realised that in view of what had happened to his mate earlier, he must err on the side of caution when on his own.

It would not go down well if he arrived on crutches for the start of his ten weeks training.

But despite his tour of the obvious places, there was no Basil Boothroyd to be seen.

He was either at home, or he'd found a new venue, then Alan reasoned, he was probably with the woman from the party.

When Alan had tried to get the dirt on what was happening there, his best friend had been very evasive. She was much older than him… and though not exactly a 'tart' but would have fitted in better at some smart London function, than at a party in the middle of nowhere. Perhaps she was new to the town, a prospective client needing some mill owner's residence that she'd just bought completely re-decorating, and Basil was being extreemly friendly and courteous for the sake of the firm – and pigs mighty fly!

No, the story would have a different slant to it than the innocent one that Alan was offering. For he knew Basil, and neither did she look the sort of woman who'd just come from a nunnery – a brothel, more like. And he'd noticed how the power behind the Boothroyd throne had re-acted on the evening of the party. The woman was definitely not welcome.

Constance Boothroyd was very good at organising her off-springs lives, selecting their friends, and such, but if she had the slightest inkling of the fortnight in Whitby then there really would be hell to do. He finished his drink, he'd have an early night. Back in the van, he switched on the headlights and started the engine. As he drove past the bus station he saw her. Wearing a bright red scarf over a dark blue coat. She was staring at the Boothroyd and Son van – he had to stop.

"Mavis," he called.

She came toward the van and peered at the driver. " 'Allo, Alan."

"You're out late. On your own?"

"Mmm. Just goin' ter catch mi bus 'ome. Ah've been ter see mi gran."

"Jump in, I'll give you a lift."

"Ooo, ta."

She settled herself beside him before asking, "An' where've you been?"

"Looking for my mate. I've tried all the usual places, but I can't find him."

"I'll bet you've lots o' mates."

"But only one real one."

"There's girls ah work wi', but," and she pulled a face, "ah don't go about wi' 'em."

"You're like me then, pretty much a loner." He stopped at the bright lights, nor did he pause to think what he was doing or saying as he blurted out, "D'you fancy a bag o' chips?" as he pointed to the takeaway.

"Ooohhh. Lovely – wi' some scraps on."

He was in a dream – this was not happening. Reality would smack him round the head later.

There was no point in mentioning his encounter with Mavis to his parents – because it had been a mistake.

A big mistake.

Here he was, a young man head over heels in love with his boss's daughter, even though she was several years older than he was, and he'd a mother and father who were prepared to do anything within their power to ensure that he didn't spend the next couple of years at some military establishment, and he himself was, after the day he'd had, beginning to have nagging doubts as to his decision. But what other alternatives were there?

Being a conscientious objector, or just pretending to be a bit simple in the head and not fit to fire a gun if called upon to do so – or working on the coal-face and going about with permanent black eyelashes, and eventually getting emphysema, or as it was referred to among those who suffered from this debilitating condition, "miner's lung".

It seemed a high price to pay for several tons of free coal each year, needing payment for transport only by the two men who regularly delivered the black diamonds around the villages for a living. "Cobblins." They called the big lumps needing two hands to lift them, and it was always delivered tipped from an open waggon, never in sacks. Five free tons a year – or was it seven he'd shovel into the coal-shed after he arrived home on "coal day."?

Life would have been very different if he'd had parents who – well, a father, anyway who was. say, a doctor, or a bank manager. It would have been a Private Education, and probably three, four years at university to gain a degree in… physics?… mathematics? Or he might have even ended up as a solicitor, a dentist – a vet – anything but a bloody painter and decorator.

But he hadn't – so there was no point in imagining what might have been.

He was little more than a labourer, and not a particularly happy one. The woman he loved had. It seemed, rejected him – and now?

Well, he must be mad to even think about the girl his father had chosen as his future wife, simply because he worked alongside her father, yet only hours earlier he and the girl concerned had been laughing and joking as they ate fish and chips together. If he were foolish enough to mention this to his parents, his dad would see it as the start of a romance leading to eventual marriage, and in due time, a couple of grandchildren. A boy and girl who would –

NO!

He must stop these daft thoughts. He needed a good night's sleep. Things would look different in the morning.

He couldn't get her out of his mind.

Not 'quite so plain' as had been his first impression… sort of… 'ordinary' perhaps. He could never truthfully describe her as beautiful, but he supposed, he was no Greek God himself. To yearn for what was obviously beyond him was foolish, as was to settle for second-best – but that all depended on how one looked at things.

Mavis Pickersgill would only seem second-best so long as he was besotted by Rosemary Boothroyd. He'd not arranged a 'date' or anything, but from their earlier conversation he knew that the visit to her gran was a weekly thing, and she always caught the same bus home. He could perhaps be casually walking through the bus station and see her, offer a lift (and fish and chips), then invite her to… say… the cinema the following weekend… and then let mum and dad know.

Or he could even do as his father had earlier suggested and make an appointment to see the manager at the pit – but he'd need to move quickly on that one before he started his ten weeks of square-bashing.

Chapter 17

His life, so it seemed to him, was getting out of control!

An invitation to Sunday afternoon tea at the Pickersgills, and interview arranged with the manager at the colliery, his mum talking about "Gettin' a new two-piece ter wear for…" and he knew she was hinting at a wedding outfit. His dad was more than friendly toward him, and Alan so hoped that he wouldn't take him to one side and give him a lecture on what was required of a groom on his wedding night.

That would be too much.

Each evening he arrived home he anticipated an official-looking letter would be waiting for him, but there was nothing. Painting and decorating had suddenly become boring, for with Basil working on the town hall contract he had no-one to banter words with, and papering front rooms and landings was not particularly inspiring when he was working on his own.

Mrs. Boothroyd now put in an appearance every day while Rosemary, still minus the single solitaire on her finger seemed to be keeping out of his way, until she suddenly surprised him by suggesting that they meet that evening to 'discuss things'.

"You mean you've – "

"This evening, Alan. We'll meet at… the Royal George. The cocktail bar, about eight-ish."

"Mmm."

There was hope for him. She'd changed her mind – well, not 'changed' her mind, but had given his earlier proposal of marriage much consideration.

It was on – she'd soon be Mrs. Beaumont.

"Yer goin' somewhere special?" his mum asked when he came downstairs in his smart suit.

"Oh… er… just a night out."

"Wi' Mavis?" his father asked, hopefully.

"No, dad. Not tonight."

"Well, 'ave a good neet. An' drive carefully."

"Don't worry, I'll be OK."

He hoped the *Old Spice* he'd doused himself with would disguise the smell of gloss paint. He'd scrubbed and better scrubbed his hands and finger nails and he sniffed them yet again. They were all right.

"I must get a move on. Don't wait up, but I'll try not to be late."

He arrived in town early, and still in the van, deliberated. A quick half somewhere – even a coffee and something to nibble? But no, he'd just take his time walking up to the hotel and… well, just take his time.

He hovered outside the entrance to the George Hotel, half expecting to see the love of his life appear, but in that he was disappointed. The weather was suddenly changing, it was coming on to rain, he had to get inside.

Cocktail bars were not really his thing, because knowing nothing about cocktails he never knew what to ask for. Bloody Mary. Pimms, Brandy Alexander, Singapore Sling – they were simply names to him, for he'd no idea what they tasted like. He only knew they tended to be served in small glasses and required large tips. Half a Guinness was better, but not quite the thing. He settled for a bottle of Lager. He glanced again at his watch. Ten minutes to eight. Soon she would be – and then he saw her in the foyer and went to meet her.

"Rosemary."

"Good evening, Alan."

"I'm over in the corner. Now, let's get you a drink."

"I think… pineapple juice, with lots of ice. I'm driving." She tried to satisfy the puzzled look on his face. "Having Basil banned from driving was bad enough, but if the police should stop me for any reason and find I've been drinking…"

"I see what you mean." He glanced at her left hand. There was no dazzling solitaire. "Well," he continued after the waiter had brought the drink, "you… er… said you 'wanted to discuss things,' Mrs. Hunter."

"Indeed. Now, where do we begin? And 'how' do we begin?"

"At the beginning?"

She gave a sigh. "Alan, I've been rehearsing this all day, and there's no easy way round it."

"You're not… well, I can see you're not wearing my ring."

"But I – "

"After our holiday I wanted to shout to the world that I loved you. I still want to do that even thought – "

"I'm pregnant?"

"Eh?"

"Well, don't look so shocked. You're going to be a father."

"Rosemary – are you sure?"

"I wouldn't make such a statement if there was any doubt, which is why we need to talk about the thing sensibly."

He stared at her, still unable to believe or comprehend her announcement.

"Well?" she quizzed him after what seemed an eternity.

"I need to take this in. When did you – I mean, you are sure, aren't you?"

She nodded.

"I'm going to be a father – I'm going to be – "

"A father!"

"Oh Rosemary, you've made me so happy. So very, very – "

"Well, I could so easily alter that. Now, what are we going to do?"

"We're going to get married right away. By… 'special licence' or whatever it's called. I know your mum would have wanted a posh do, but we can't help that. By the way, what does she say?"

"She doesn't know."

He could imagine exactly what she'd say, and when Basil found out, well, he'd beat the living daylights out of him. Be better if he could be doing his ten weeks square bashing before the news broke, but under the circumstances – and what about his own mum and dad? How would they re-act? They'd not even met Rosemary, but were now ready to welcome Mavis as part of the family, and expect him to be working alongside his father and possibly father-in-law on the coalface.

Everything – just about bloody everything was happening in his life and he seemed powerless to prevent or control it. He looked again at the bearer of – well, was it 'good news'? It would depend on how Rosemary herself viewed it. Finally, he spoke.

"Rosemary, you know I love you, don't you? I wouldn't have given you the solitaire if I hadn't been serious in my intentions. And now? Well, I want to be a proper father when our baby's born. I want us to be husband and wife, and I'll do whatever you want to help make this happen. If it's doing National Service and us being parted for eighteen months then that will pass, we'll have the rest of our lives together, or I'll even go down the pit and work with dad, then I'll be here to help when the time comes. Have you thought of a name for him yet? What about Stephen? – or Mark? Yes, that sounds good. Mark Beaumont."

"For God's sake, Alan! It might be easier if this pregnancy was terminated. It's illegal, but there are ways round these things. You know, some fancy specialist, seen 'privately' of course could say that having this child could seriously damage my health. Therefore – "

"You'd kill our baby?"

"It's not a 'baby' yet – and do keep your voice down. That's why I arranged for us to have this discussions in front of people. We can't let our emotions get the better of us."

"Please, Rosemary… don't do anything hastily that you'll regret later. As I said you weeks ago, I'm not a millionaire, but I can give you something that far outweighs money, I can give you love. I can be a good father and help you bring up our little boy, or girl, whichever."

There was a long silence as the mother-to-be pondered on his words. Finally, she spoke. "I accept that I'm several years older than you, and I'm having your child. When the baby's born I could manage financially without you having to pay a penny in maintenance, And I don't want you to feel in any way 'trapped', but you see… I love you." She gave a long sigh. "There, I've said it. I love you!"

"Well then, let's go to the Registrar tomorrow lunchtime and get a date fixed. The sooner the better. Er… should we tell our parents before or after we do the deed, so to speak?"

She pulled a face and shrugged her shoulders. "Mum will not be pleased – about the baby, that is, but she has to know."

"I want to be with you when you tell her. I want to protect you, take the blame, if you like. And when Basil gets to know – God, there'll be hell to do."

"I thought you were the best of friends."

"Oh. We are. But if he imagines I've seduced and ruined his twin sister, he might want revenge."

"He's too engrossed at the moment with seeing this woman he brought to the party. Seeing 'far too much' of her, so mother claims."

"Oh yes – who is she, by the way?"

"Someone mother's taken a dislike to – but that's not unusual in it, knowing my mother."

"I hope she doesn't do that to me, when she finds out."

"But you're marrying me, not mother," and from her handbag, Rosemary took out the box containing the engagement ring and handed it to him. Like lovesick suitors he had seen in so many movies he knelt down on one knee, and in full view of the somewhat surprised patrons of the Royal George Hotel cocktail bar, looked into her eyes and said simply, "Rosemary, will you marry me?"

She held out her left hand and with much bravado he slipped the single solitaire on her third finger.

Chapter 18

"But this is outrageous. You should be locked away for getting our daughter pregnant. And when exactly did this rape, and I can only describe it as that, take place?"

"Constance, do try to calm down. The damage is done."

"Calm down?" she screamed at her husband. "Your daughter tells us she's pregnant and the animal responsible is no more than a labourer, an employee of yours – and you ask me to calm down?"

"Well, what can we do about it?"

"We can dismiss him to start with, and we can also make that no other firm of decorators within fifty miles will employ him. Then we can go and see his parents and – "

"Mother, this isn't solving anything, and really, there's nothing to 'solve'. We're in love, and we're getting married by special – "

"Oh no, young lady. When you get married – and it will not be to this 'nobody', it will be the social event of the year. Pictures and write-ups in the leading Yorkshire magazines, and it will be to a man who care for you financially and support you in the manner to which you've been accustomed to."

"But what about our baby?"

She stared at him. "There'll be no 'baby.' You go and do eighteen months… two years in the army and just forget the mess you've caused. 'Things' can be arranged, and she turned to her daughter. "Trust me, Rosemary. I really do have your interests at heart."

"But not the baby's."

Her hand came across the father-to-be's face. "Get out," she screamed, "before I get the police to throw you out."

He recoiled from the blow, as her husband held her off before she could inflict any more harm. "Don't forget, we have friends in very high places."

"Oh, not that again, Constance," her husband tried to calm down the volatile situation. "Let's… try to think this thing through. Alan here has had the guts to admit he's responsible, and a lot of young fellers in his position wouldn't. He prepared, and wanting to do the right thing by both our daughter and their unborn child," and he thought of his own misspent youth and the love-child he'd fathered but had not had the guts or the decency to own up to.

"And what about the scandal this will cause? Having a son who's consorting with filth is bad enough, but an un-married daughter pregnant, and the man responsible in the army and miles away – and when he gets out of the way we'll never hear from him again. Who then will want to look at a woman in her thirties with a bastard child? Who in his right mind would want to wed her? Answer me that."

"But you're overlooking the most important thing. We love one another – and we're getting married."

"Not if I have anything to do with it – and have the manners to remember who, and where you are, young man. You're nothing more than an employee. A common – very common tradesman, and you're in our home. This is not a back-to-back row of miners hovels, it's – "

"Constance, shut up!"

She spun round on her husband. "Don't you dare tell me to 'Shut up'."

"Then stop being so bloody rude. Now," and he turned to the father-to-be, "what have your mum and dad to say about this?"

"They don't know – well, I didn't know myself until a couple of hours ago."

"How do you think they'll react?"

"Does that matter?" his wife again took up arms. "Being common as muck, it'll be no scandal to them."

"Mrs. Boothroyd, say nasty things about me all you like, but not about my parents. They have nothing to do with this. In fact, they've never met Rosemary, but when they do meet her and we tell them that she's having my child they'll be much more loving and caring than you appear to be."

"Of course they will – marrying into a well-to-do family."

"Mother, you've said enough tonight. I can't stand any more of your nasty, spiteful remarks. I'm going to bed. Goodnight Alan, and we'll do as we've planned tomorrow lunchtime."

"Right. I'll leave now, Rosemary. Goodnight to you all."

"And when Basil hears of this – well, I wouldn't want to be in your shoes."

"Goodnight, Mrs. Boothroyd." He wanted to say "Get on your broomstick," but thought better of it.

It was an uneventful drive home. Very little traffic on the road and certainly no pedestrians. The house was in darkness, the night air tore at his throat as he walked toward the front door. He made a quick mug of instant coffee and minutes later was hanging his suit in the wardrobe, and putting out his clothes for the following day. He'd need a decent shirt and tie, and his sports jacket? He'd need to look fairly smart for going to the registrar's office.

He deliberated.

Should he tell his parents before he left for work, or wait until the deed had been done – but either way they'd need to know, and soon. His life seemed to be getting even more out of control, and he was powerless to prevent whatever fate threw at him.

It was a restless night. He woke early.

A scary dawn was breaking – another traumatic day was about to begin.

www.ingramcontent.com/pod-product-compliance
Ingram Content Group UK Ltd.
Pitfield, Milton Keynes, MK11 3LW, UK
UKHW020240250726
13967UKWH00001B/467